"If you tell me what you're looking for I might be able to help?"
A voice, low and gravelly, had emerged from the heaped-up quilt.

Then more of the man emerged as he propped himself up on one arm. Naked shoulders, a naked chest with a splattering of dark hair that arrowed down to a hard, flat stomach....

"Um...." Ginny murmured, mesmerised.

"I'm sorry?" One of Richard Mallory's brows kinked upwards. "I didn't quite catch that."

She swallowed hard. There was nothing to do but bluff it out and hope for the best.

"I was looking for my hamster."

Dear Reader,

Quiet, studious Ginny Lautour and Sophie Harrington, privileged, lively, the natural class "princess," were the two girls least likely to be friends. But Sophie's natural kindness in rescuing a lost soul on her first day at school and clever Ginny's aptitude for getting Sophie out of trouble forged the kind of bond that lasts a lifetime. So when Sophie begs for Ginny's help to save her job, even though it means breaking into her sexy billionaire playboy neighbor's apartment, she doesn't hesitate.

And everything would have been fine if Richard Mallory was—as promised—away for the weekend. But then Sophie wasn't being entirely honest with her best friend. She wasn't in trouble. Just matchmaking!

As Sophie discovers, however, when you tell a big fat fib, even if it is with the best of intentions, it's likely to come back and bite you. Homeless, jobless and with Ginny honeymooning with her beloved Richard, Sophie has no one to turn to. For the first time ever she has to live on what she can earn and, with Christmas coming, the only job on offer is that of dog walker to gorgeous grouch Gabriel York. But it's the season for miracles and once he offers her a home, no matter how temporary, all things are possible.

I do hope you enjoy reading how best friends Ginny and Sophie find their very special happy endings in *The Billionaire Takes a Bride* and *A Surprise Christmas Proposal*.

With love,

Liz

THE BILLIONAIRE TAKES A BRIDE

LIZ FIELDING

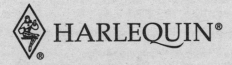

HARLEQUIN®

TORONTO • NEW YORK • LONDON
AMSTERDAM • PARIS • SYDNEY • HAMBURG
STOCKHOLM • ATHENS • TOKYO • MILAN • MADRID
PRAGUE • WARSAW • BUDAPEST • AUCKLAND

For the ladies of the eHarlequin Writers' Auxiliary and Hamster Circle. Thanks for the laughs.

ISBN 0-373-18163-9

THE BILLIONAIRE TAKES A BRIDE

First North American Publication 2004.

Copyright © 2003 by Liz Fielding.

This edition published by arrangement with Harlequin Books S.A.

® and TM are trademarks of the publisher. Trademarks indicated with ® are registered in the United States Patent and Trademark Office, the Canadian Trade Marks Office and in other countries.

www.eHarlequin.com

Printed in U.S.A.

CHAPTER ONE

THIS was a mistake. A big mistake. Every cell in Ginny's body was slamming on the brakes, digging in its heels, trying to claw its way back behind the safety of the rain-soaked hedge that divided her roof top terrace from the raked perfection of Richard Mallory's Japanese garden, with its mossy rocks, carp pool and paper-walled pavilion.

Previous perfection.

Her boots had left deep impressions in the damp gravel. So much for stealth.

She was not cut out for burglary. Even her clothes were wrong. She should have been in svelte black and wearing light-weight tennis shoes that made no noise, her hair bolted down under a tight ski cap...

Oh, for heaven's sake. It was the middle of the morning and the last thing she wanted to look like was a burglar.

In the unlikely event that she was discovered it was important that she looked exactly what she was. A distressed neighbour looking for her lost pet...

Somebody totally innocent. And an innocent person didn't change shoes, or happen to be wearing the appropriate clothing to battle through a hedge. Her lace-ups, baggy jeans and a loose shirt in an eye-gouging purple—fifty pence from her favourite charity shop—screamed innocent. Of everything except bad taste.

She groaned.

Distressed was right.

She had promised herself that she would never volunteer to do anything like this ever again. Not even for Sophie. Famous last words.

Her mouth hadn't been paying attention.

She took a deep steadying breath and firmly beat back the urgent desire to bolt. It would be fine. She had every angle covered and this was for a friend. A friend in trouble.

A friend who was always in trouble.

A friend who'd always been there for her, she reminded herself.

She took another deep breath, then stepped through the open French windows into the empty room.

'Er, hello?'

Her voice emerged as a painful croak. A bit like a frog with laryngitis. She had her story all ready in the unlikely event that someone answered, but that didn't stop her heart from pounding like the entire timpani section of the London Philharmonic…

'Anyone home?'

The only response was the faint whirr of a washing machine hitting the spin cycle.

Apart from that no sound of any kind.

No turning back.

She had fifteen minutes. Maybe twenty if she was lucky. A brief window of opportunity while the cleaner, having opened up the French windows to let in the fresh air, as she did every morning—why had she mentioned that to Sophie?—and put on the washing, was downstairs flirting with the hall porter over a cup of coffee.

Okay. She wiped the sweat from her upper lip. She could do this. Fifteen minutes was more than enough time to find one little computer disk and save stupid Sophie's stupid job.

Excuse me? Who exactly is the stupid one here?

The prod from her subconscious was unnecessary. She was the one burgling her neighbour's apartment while 'stupid'

Sophie was safely at work, surrounded by an office full of alibi-providing colleagues. Should the need for one arise.

While quiet, sensible Ginny—who should at this moment be safely tucked up in the British Library researching Homeric myths—was the one who'd be arrested.

All the more reason not to waste any more time wool-gathering. Even so, she took a moment to look around, get her bearings. This was not the moment to knock something over…

Mallory's penthouse apartment, like his garden, tended towards the minimalist. There was very little furniture—but all of it so perfectly simple that you just knew it had cost a mint—a few exquisite pieces of modern ceramics and absolutely acres of pale polished wood floor.

Stay well away from the ceramics, she told herself. Don't go near the ceramics…

There was only one 'off' note.

Spotlit by a beam of sunlight that had found its way through the scudding clouds, a black silk stocking tied in a neat bow around the neck of a champagne bottle next to two champagne flutes looked shockingly decadent in such an austere setting.

A linen napkin—on which something

had been scrawled in what looked like lip-stick—was tucked into the bow.

A thank you note?

She swallowed hard and firmly quashing her curiosity—she was in enough trouble already—resisted the temptation to take a look.

Whatever it said, the scene confirmed everything she'd heard about the man's reputation. Not his reputation as a genius, or money machine. Those went without saying. The financial papers regularly gen-uflected to his brilliance while salivating over Mallory plc's profits.

It was his reputation as a babe magnet that seemed to be confirmed by this still-life-with-champagne tableau.

Despite being his next door neighbour, albeit on a temporary basis, their paths hadn't yet crossed so she'd had no oppor-tunity to check this out for herself. Not that she was the kind of 'babe' he'd look at twice—she wasn't any kind of 'babe', as she'd be the first to acknowledge.

Whether or not he magnetised her.

Not that he would. Magnetise her.

No matter how superficially attractive, she didn't find anything appealing about a man who had a reputation for casual affairs, even if the gossip columns loved him for it. But then she didn't think much of gossip columns, either.

She pushed her spectacles up her nose and, putting her hand over her heart in an effort to cut down on the jack-hammer noise it was making, made a big effort to concentrate on what Sophie had told her.

He'd taken the disk home with him earlier in the week and it would be lying about on his desk somewhere. Probably.

Totally confident of her ability to find the thing—'I mean, how difficult could it be?'—Sophie had been weak on actual details.

About as weak as her reason for not doing this herself. If this was such a breeze, why couldn't she squeeze through the rain-soaked hedge—the very *prickly* rain-soaked hedge—and get it herself? After all, she only lived a few floors down, in the same apartment block.

'But darling, you're living next door to the man. It's just so perfect. Almost as if it was fate. If he even suspects I was anywhere near his study I'll not only lose my job, I'll never get another one. The man's a complete bastard. He has absolutely no

tolerance for anything less than perfection...'

Right. Of course. She remembered now. Sophie couldn't risk getting caught. The whole point was to save her job. The only mystery was why she was working for a computer software company in the first place. She usually preferred a little light PR work, or swanning about looking decorative in an art gallery...

Sophie had made it all sound so simple. A quick trip through the hedge that divided her roof garden from his and Bob, apparently, would be her uncle. Which was why Ginny had been nominated to ransack this 'complete bastard's' apartment, 'borrow' the disk, copy and return it—thus saving Sophie's job—without his ever knowing she'd been there.

Piece of cake.

A low groan escaped her lips. She wasn't built for burglary. Or was it breaking and entering? When she hadn't actually broken in?

A fine legal point that she was sure the magistrate would explain as he passed sentence if she didn't find the disk and get out of there before Mrs Figgis returned from her daily dalliance over a double *latte* with the porter.

Unfortunately, although she was sending urgent 'move' messages from her brain to her feet, her synapses appeared to be on a go-slow. Or maybe they were just frozen with terror like the rest of her.

Never again, she vowed, as the message finally got through and her feet came un-stuck from the spot to which she had been glued for what seemed like hours. This was positively, absolutely, totally the last time she would allow Sophie Harrington to talk her into trouble.

No. That was unfair. She'd managed to talk herself into trouble. But who could re-sist Sophie Harrington when she turned on the charm?

Twenty-four years old going on fifteen.

This was just like Ginny's raid on the school secretary's office all over again. That time it had been Sophie's life-or-death need to reclaim her diary before the head-mistress read it. Only an idiot would carry such an inflammatory document around with her. Only a complete idiot would be stupid enough to write it in class...

Except that on this occasion if she got caught pulling her best friend's irons from the fire she risked a lot more than a shocked 'I expected better from you' lecture and a suspension of visits to the village for the rest of the term.

She dragged her mind back to reality. Cloakroom, kitchen… She came to a stunned halt as she took in the brushed steel and slate wonder of Mallory's state-of-the-art kitchen. What couldn't she do in a kitchen like that?

Richard Mallory wouldn't need to use magnets on her, she decided, just offer her the run of his kitchen…

For heaven's sake! She had less than fifteen minutes and she was wasting them drooling over his top of the range knives!

She moved quickly across the room and opened a door on the far side of the two-storey-high living space. Desk, laptop… Bingo!

Good grief, it looked as if a madman had been working without cease for a week. In contrast to everywhere else that had looked almost unlived in. Apart, that was, from the champagne bottle and flutes. One of them barely touched.

So, which of them had been in too much of a hurry…?

She really didn't want to think about that

and, dragging her mind back to the study, decided that untidy was good. It meant he probably wouldn't be obsessive about locking stuff away.

It also meant there was a lot to look through. Empty water bottles, chocolate bar wrappers—he had seriously good taste in chocolate—and a ton of paper covered with figures littering the desk and floor.

Unfortunately, once she'd looked under all the papers, she could see that was all there was. Not a disk in sight.

She dragged her wandering mind back into line and tried the desk drawers. They didn't budge. So much for the casual-about-security theory. And the key would be with him, on his long weekend in the country. Along with the owner of the black silk stocking.

Although, if that was the case, why the note? She jerked her curiosity back into line.

Why on earth would she care?

She checked her watch. Six precious minutes gone…

Okay. Keys came in sets of two so there had to be a spare somewhere. She ran her fingers beneath the desk, under the drawers, in case it was taped there. Well, no. First place a burglar would look, obviously. Even a first time burglar like her.

If you didn't count the school secretary's office…

Where would she keep the spare key to her desk drawer?

Safely in the drawer so she wouldn't lose it, but then she didn't have anything worth locking up. Okay, there were files and disks containing months of painstaking research. Nothing anyone would want to steal, though. But supposing she did…

In her bedside drawer seemed a likely place. Who would ever find it amongst all the clutter?

But would a man think that way? What did men put in their bedside drawers, anyway?

She had no way of knowing but, short of any other ideas, she abandoned the study and ran up the spiral staircase to the upper floor, emerging in a wide gallery where comfort had been allowed to encroach on the severity of the minimalist theme.

The floor was covered with a lovely old Turkish rug, there was a huge, much used leather armchair and the walls were lined, floor to ceiling, with shelves crammed with books that looked as if they'd been read, rather than arranged by an expensive decorator just for effect. She moved towards them on automatic, stumbling over a low table she hadn't noticed and sending a heap of magazines slithering to the floor.

The noise was horrendous. But it brought her back to her senses. This was no time for browsing...

There was only one door leading from the gallery. Rubbing her shin, she opened it, stepping into a wide inner hallway lit from above by a series of skylights and groaned as she was confronted by half a dozen doors, opening the doors to an airing cupboard and two guest suites before she finally found Mallory's room. It had to be his room. It was in darkness, the heavy curtains still shut tight against the feeble morning sunlight.

She left the door open to give her some light and looked around. There was very little furniture, which rather confused her.

The whole apartment was so different from the McBrides' which, like the apartment block that Sir William had designed, had an art deco feel to it. Even the garden.

But it seemed that Mallory's taste for minimalism extended even to his sleeping arrangements. A very low—and very large—unmade bed dominated the room. Mounded up with a mountainous quilt and pillows and flanked by a pair of equally low tables, each with a tall lamp.

She crossed quickly to the nearest one. At first, she couldn't work out how to open the narrow, flush-fitting drawer. The lamp would have helped, but her hands were shaking so much with nerves that she was sure to knock it flying if she attempted to switch it on.

Instead, she got down on her knees and felt underneath, relieved to discover that the trick to it was nothing more complicated than a finger ledge.

She pulled and discovered the answer to her question. The drawer contained a quantity of products that suggested Richard Mallory was a man whose guiding principle in life was 'be prepared'.

Frequently.

She closed it quickly. Okay. Enough was enough. She was running out of time here. And Sophie was running out of luck. She'd check the other table so that she could say she had done everything possible. After that, she was out of there.

Then, as she began to get to her feet, something caught her eye. A glint of something small and shiny under the table, right up against the wall, that might be a key. For a moment she was torn. What was the likelihood that this was the key she was looking for?

But then it had to fit something...

She had to lie down and stretch out flat before she could reach it. It felt right—long and narrow—and she emerged, flushed from the effort as she backed out, holding up the object to get a better look. Light, she needed more light. As she reached for the lamp it came on by itself. Startled, she stared at it for a moment, then grinned. That was so brilliant! She'd heard of lamps that did that...

But this was not the time to investigate. She turned her attention back to the small metallic object she'd picked up. 'Oh, drat...'

'Not one of yours, I take it?'

The voice, low and gravelly, had emerged from the heaped-up quilt, along with a mop of dark, tousled hair and a pair of heavy-lidded eyes. It was followed by a hand which tossed aside a remote and lifted the sliver of platinum from her open palm and, warm fingers brushing against her neck, held it up against her ear.

Not a key, but an earring. Long, slender...

And that was just his fingers.

'No,' he said, after looking at it and then at her for what seemed like an age, during which her heart took a unilateral decision not to beat—probably something to do with all the magnetism flowing from those electric blue eyes—before dropping it back into her hand. 'Not your style.'

A sound—something incoherent that might have been agreement—emerged from Ginny's throat. Recycled charity shop was cheap. That was its attraction. Whether it could be described as a style...

'If you tell me what you're looking for I might be able to help?' he prompted.

More of Richard Mallory emerged from beneath the quilt as he propped himself up on one arm. Naked shoulders, a naked chest with a spattering of dark hair that arrowed down to a hard, flat stomach...

'Um...' she murmured, mesmerised.

'I'm sorry?' One brow kinked upward. 'I didn't quite catch that.'

The sleepy lids were deceptive. His eyes, she realised, were wide awake. How long had he been watching her? Had he witnessed her attack on his bedside drawer?

She swallowed hard. There was nothing to do but bluff it out and hope for the best. If she could handle a room full of eighteen-year-old undergraduates who thought they knew it all—and who almost certainly knew a lot more than her about pretty much anything other than Greek myth—she could surely handle one man...

As his eyes continued to burn into her, she decided she'd take the lecture hall any day. Unfortunately, it wasn't an option. Bluff would have to do it.

'I said, ''um'',' she replied, pushing her glasses up her nose as she found her 'teacher' voice. After all he couldn't sack *her*...

He could, of course, call the police.

'Um?' He repeated the word back at her as if it was from some foreign language. One he'd never before encountered.

Bluff, bluff.

It was easy. She did it all the time. It was how she had got through the lectures she had given to help support herself through her doctorate. All she had to do, she reminded herself, was use the classic technique of imagining that he was naked. From what she'd seen so far she wasn't finding it difficult. He probably *was* naked...

Oh, bad idea.

Think of something else. Her mother...

'Not the acme of clear thought translated into speech—' she said, her thoughts—and vocal cords—snapping right back into line '—but then you did startle me, Mr Mallory.'

This, for some reason, appeared to entertain him. 'Do you expect me to apologise?'

'That really isn't necessary.' She finally wrenched her gaze from the wide expanse of his shoulders and, scrambling to her feet, put a little distance between them. 'It's entirely my fault, after all. I didn't realise you were here, or I wouldn't have just...' Her desperate attempt to appear cool in a difficult situation buckled under his undisguised amusement. He was, she realised belatedly, teasing her...

'Just?' he prompted.

'Um...' That foreign word again...

'Just um?'

'I wouldn't have just walked in,' she snapped. Then, because that seemed to lack something, she said, 'I'd have knocked first.'

'Really?' His eyebrows suggested he was seriously surprised. 'That would be a first.'

She frowned, confused, unable to drag her gaze from his shoulders. Or the way the muscle, emphasized by deep shadows, bunched up as he shrugged.

Then she realised what he was implying and felt herself blush. Of all the arrogant, self-opinionated… She wasn't some Richard Mallory 'groupie', intent on flinging herself on his irresistible body!

'If it's a regular problem maybe you should keep your bedroom door locked,' she advised, perhaps more sharply than was wise under the circumstances.

'Maybe I should,' he agreed. Then, bringing her back to the point, 'So? What *were* you looking for?'

Her heart—which was having a seriously bad morning—skipped a beat. She should have legged it while she had the chance, instead of sticking around to chat. He might have dismissed the whole incident as a bad dream. She'd had worse nightmares.

'Looking for?' she repeated.

'Under my bed.'

'Oh.'

Help…

Her excuse had sounded perfectly reasonable as she'd rehearsed it in the safety of her own apartment. But then she'd never expected to have to use it. She'd be in and out in a flash, Sophie had promised.

When would she ever learn?

What had sounded reasonable as a back-up story, in the event that the cleaner returned early from her morning flirtation with the porter, lacked any real credibility when confronted with the man himself.

Or maybe it was just guilt turning the words to ashes in her mouth.

That was silly.

It wasn't as if she was a *real* burglar, for heaven's sake. She was only going to borrow the disk—it would be back on his desk before he'd missed it. Hardly a matter for the Crown Court.

Unless, of course, she killed Sophie.

'In your own time,' he encouraged.

Faced with a pair of sharp blue eyes that suggested Richard Mallory would not be so easy to flannel as a 'daily' with dalliance on her mind, that seemed a very attractive idea. Right now, however, she had a more pressing problem and she trawled her brain in a desperate attempt to come up with a story that was just a little less…ridiculous.

.Her brain had, apparently, taken the day off.

But then why else would she be here?

Please, please, she prayed, let the floor open up and swallow me now. The floor refused to oblige.

She was out of time and stuck with the excuse she'd prepared earlier.

'I was looking for my hamster,' she said.

'Excuse me?' He laughed. 'Did you say your *hamster*?'

Faced with his amusement she felt a certain irritation. A need to defend her story. It wasn't *that* ridiculous.

Okay, so maybe it was. A kitten would have been cuter, but the cleaner would have known she didn't have a kitten. Nothing uncaged was allowed within the portals of Chandler's Reach.

'He escaped,' she said. 'He made a break for it through the hedge and headed straight for your French windows.' And when this didn't elicit polite concern... 'It took me longer to get through it. He's smaller,' she elaborated when Mallory remained silent. 'He was able to scoot underneath.' Then, in desperation, 'It's really scratchy...'

She could not believe she was saying this. Richard Mallory's expression suggested he was having problems with it too, but was making a manful effort not to laugh out loud.

In an attempt to distract him, she took a step closer and extended her hand.

'We haven't met, Mr Mallory, but we're temporarily neighbours. I'm Iphegenia Lautour.' Only the most truthful person in the entire world would own up to a name like that voluntarily, right? 'I'm looking after Sir William and Lady McBride's apartment. For the summer. Next door,' she added, in case he didn't know his neighbours. 'While they're away. Flat-sitting. You know—dusting the whatnot, watering the houseplants. Feeding the goldfish,' she added. Then, as if there was nothing at all out of the ordinary in the situation, she said, 'How d'you do?'

'I think—' he said, looking slightly nonplussed as he took her hand, gripping it firmly for a moment, holding it for longer than was quite necessary '—that I need notice of that question.'

He sat up, leaned forward and raked his hands through his hair, as if somehow he could straighten out his thoughts along with his unruly curls.

It did nothing for the curls, but the sight

of his naked shoulders, a chest spattered with exactly the right amount of dark hair, left her with an urgent need to swallow.

He dragged his hands down over his face. 'Along with coffee, orange juice and a shower. In no particular order of preference. I've had a hard night.'

Ginny didn't doubt it. She'd seen the evidence for herself...

She gave a little squeak as he flung back the covers and swung his feet to the floor. Backed hurriedly away. Knocked the lamp, grabbed to stop it from falling and only made things worse, flinched as it hit the carpet.

Mallory stood up, reached down and set it back on the table, giving her plenty of time to see that he wasn't, after all, totally naked but wearing a pair of soft grey shorts.

Naked enough. They clung to his hips by the skin of their teeth, exposing a firm flat belly and leaving little else to the imagination.

It was definitely time to get out of there.

'I'm disturbing you,' she said, groping behind her for the door handle but succeeding only in pushing the door shut. With her on the wrong side.

'You could say that,' he agreed, picking up the remote and using it to draw back the curtains so that daylight flooded into the room.

'Neat trick,' she said. 'Is that how you turned on the light?' It was a mistake to draw attention to herself because he turned those searching blue eyes on her.

One of them was definitely disturbed.

'I'm really sorry—'

'Don't be,' he said, cutting off her apology. 'I'd have slept all day if you hadn't woken me. Iphegenia?' he prompted, with a frown. 'What kind of name is that?'

'The kind that no one can spell?' she offered. Then, 'My mother's a classical scholar,' she added—at least she was, when she could spare the time—as if that explained everything. He looked blank. 'Iphegenia was the daughter of King Agamemnon. He sacrificed her to the gods in return for a fair wind to Troy. So that he could grab back his runaway sister-in-law. Helen.'

'Helen?' he repeated. If not dumb, definitely founded...

'Of Troy.'

'Oh, right, ''...the face that launched a

thousand ships and burnt the topless towers of Ilium''?'

'That's the one,' she said. Then, 'He got murdered by his wife for his trouble. But you probably knew that.' There was more, a lot more, but years of explaining her unusual name had taught her that was about as much as anyone wanted to know. 'Homer was writing about the dysfunctional family nearly three thousand years ago,' she offered.

'Yes.' He looked, for a moment, as if he might pursue her mother's choice of name... Then, thinking better of it, said, 'Tell me about your wandering hamster. What's *his* name? Odysseus?'

Irony. He'd just woken up and he could quote Christopher Marlowe, recall the names of mythical heroes and do irony. Impressive.

But then he *was* a genius.

'Good try, but a bit of a mouthful for a hamster, don't you think?' she asked, keeping her mouth busy while her mind did some fast footwork.

'I'd say Iphegenia is a bit of a mouthful for a girl,' he said, as if he knew she was simply playing for time. 'The kind of name that suggests your mother was not feeling particularly warm towards your father when she gave it to you. If I gave it any serious thought.'

He wasn't even close.

'So what is this runaway rodent called?' he asked when she made no comment, pushing her for an answer.

'Hector,' she said.

'Hector? Not Harry—as in Houdini?'

No, Hector. As in heroic Trojan warrior prince slain by Achilles. Classical scholarship ran in the family but she thought she'd probably said more than enough on that subject.

'Harry who?' she asked innocently.

His eyes narrowed and for a moment she was afraid she'd gone too far. 'Never mind,' he said, letting it go. 'He must be quite a mover if you chased him up here. Didn't the stairs slow him down?'

She hadn't thought of that. Hadn't thought, full stop. Certainly hadn't even considered the possibility that Richard Mallory would be at home in bed recovering from a hot date instead of where he was supposed to be, in deepest Gloucestershire.

Thank you, Sophie...

She supposed she should be grateful that

the woman with the black silk stockings wasn't under the duvet with him. Although she would at least have offered a distraction.

Ginny attempted to recall exactly how large hamsters were. Four or five inches, perhaps, at full stretch? And she realised she was so deep in trouble that the only possibility of escape was to keep on digging in the hope of eventually tunnelling out.

'Hector—' she said, with a conviction she was far from feeling '—has thighs like a footballer. It's all that running on his exercise wheel.' Then, 'Look, I'd better go—' before his brain was fully engaged and he began to ask questions to which she had no answer '—and, um, let you have your shower.'

'Oh, please, don't rush off.'

He was across the room before she could escape, his hand flat against the door, towering over her as she backed up hard against it in an attempt to put some space between them so that he wouldn't feel the wild, nervous hammering of her heart.

In an attempt to avoid the magnetic pull of his body.

'I so rarely encounter this level of entertainment before breakfast.'

CHAPTER TWO

RICHARD MALLORY'S chest, those heroic shoulders, the warm male scent of his flesh, was making it very hard to breathe normally. A fact she was sure he knew only too well.

'I—um—'

'Why don't you stay and join me?'

Join him?

With one hand keeping the door firmly shut, he used the other to deal with a wayward strand of hair that had been dragged from its scrunchy as she'd fought her way through the hedge and was now slowly descending across her face.

It wasn't just his eyes that generated electricity. Her skin fizzed, tightened at his touch and not just on her cheek, her temple. Her entire body reacted as if it had been jump-started like some long dead battery.

No. Not long dead. Never charged.

'Join you?' she repeated, stupidly.

Did he mean in the shower?

Why didn't that sound like a totally impossible idea? And what on earth was he doing to her hair?

She flattened herself against the door, moved her mouth in an attempt to form a coherent sentence. Something along the lines of What the hell do you think you're doing? should do it. No, it would have to be something simpler. Stop...

He plucked a twig from her hair, holding it up for her inspection. 'I hope you didn't do Her Ladyship's perfectly clipped hedge mortal damage.' Then, without waiting for her to elaborate on the extent of the mayhem she'd caused in Lady McBride's exquisite formal roof terrace, 'I won't be more than five minutes. Stay and tell me all about your athletic pet over some scrambled eggs—'

Five minutes? Eggs? Then reality sunk in.

'Eggs?' she repeated. 'You meant join you for breakfast?'

His mouth widened in a lazy smile that deepened the lines bracketing his mouth.

'What else?'

Her own mouth worked soundlessly for a moment before she finally managed to engage teeth and tongue and exclaim, 'Are you serious?' And feigning blank astonishment—which wasn't difficult, blank perfectly described the state of her mind—she covered her blushes by snatching the twig from him and stuffing it into her pocket. 'I had breakfast hours ago. It's nearly lunchtime. I shouldn't be here at all. I should be working...'

'Plants to water, whatnots to dust...?'

'A woman's work...' she agreed, leaving him to complete the saying. It wasn't politically correct—her mother would have been shocked that she could even think such thoughts. But her mother wasn't here to criticise and right at that moment she'd have said anything to escape...

All she had to do was move. All she had to do was remember how.

'How did the McBrides find you?' he asked while she was still thinking about it.

'Find me?' She hadn't been lost... 'Oh, I see. It was a personal introduction. I know their daughter-in-law. Philly. Slightly,' she added. She wasn't claiming any deep personal friendship. 'She knew I needed somewhere to stay in London for the summer and they needed someone...'

'To feed the goldfish?'

'Look, I'd better go.'

But he wasn't quite finished with her.

'Aren't you forgetting something?'

'Am I?'

'Hector?' he prompted. 'Surely you're not going to abandon him?'

Drat with knobs on.

'He could be anywhere,' she offered just a little desperately, discovering too late that a make-believe pet could be as much trouble as a real one. 'He'll have found himself a quiet corner and gone to sleep by now.' He was beginning to assume a presence and character all his own. 'They're nocturnal, you know.' She swallowed. 'H-hamsters.'

'Is that a fact? Then I'll be sure not to make too much noise. He must be tired after all that effort.' And he finally straightened, releasing her from his personal force field which had held her fixed to the spot far more effectively than any door. When she still didn't move he said, 'Well, if you're sure I can't tempt you...'

'No!' Did that sound too vehement? She was beyond caring. 'I really do have to go.'

'If you insist.' He made a gesture that suggested she was free to leave any time. 'It's been a pleasure meeting you, Iphegenia Lautour.'

He was laughing at her now and not making any real attempt to hide the fact. But that was okay. She'd been laughed at before and this was the warm, teasing kind that didn't hurt. In fact, she was beginning to wonder if Sophie had misjudged him. He might be a shocking flirt, but he did seem to have the redeeming feature of a well-developed sense of humour...

'Ginny,' she said, her voice no longer crisp but unusually thick and soft.

It seemed to go with the tingling in her breasts, a curious weakness in her thighs. He had the most kissable mouth of any man she'd ever met, she decided. Not that she'd met many men she would cross the road to kiss.

Firm, wide, the lower lip a sensual invitation to help herself...

She caught her own lower lip between her teeth before she did something truly stupid, cooling it with her tongue.

'People call me Ginny,' she explained. 'Usually. It's shorter.'

'And easier to spell.' The muscles at the side of his jaw clenched briefly. Then, since she was clearly rooted to the spot, he opened the door and held it wide for her.

'I'll keep a look out for Hector, Ginny, and if I find him I'll be sure to send him home.'

She was being dismissed. A minute ago she was desperate to escape. Now he was reduced to encouraging her to leave.

'If Mrs Figgis, your cleaner—' she added in case he wasn't personally acquainted with the lady who kept his apartment free of dust '—doesn't suck him up in her vacuum cleaner thinking he's a lump of fluff,' she said, before she could stop herself. Her urgent desire to flee evaporating the moment a swift exit offered itself.

'Perhaps you'd better warn her,' he suggested.

'I will. And I'm, um, really sorry for disturbing you.'

'I wouldn't have—' he paused, smiled '—um…missed it for the world. But now I really must take that shower, so unless you want to come and keep an eye on me, make sure I don't drown the heroic Hector…' He stood back, offering her a clear route to his bathroom.

This time there was no hiding the crimson tide that swept from her neck to her hairline as she finally caught on to what he already knew. That she'd become just one more case of iron filings clinging to his personal magnet.

'No...' She backed through the door, raising her hand, palm up, in a self-protective little gesture. 'Really, Mr Mallory, I trust you.'

'Rich,' he said. 'People call me Rich.'

'Yes,' she mumbled. 'I know. I've seen it in the papers...'

Then she turned and fled.

Ginny couldn't believe she'd just blundered into a strange man's bedroom then lied shamelessly while he flirted with her. Worse, that she'd responded as if he'd reached out and flipped a switch—turning her on had been that easy. And, with the game so swiftly won, he'd lived up to his reputation and just as quickly become bored.

She groaned as she ran down the spiral staircase, wishing that it were possible to stop the clock, rewind time...

'Miss Lautour?' Mrs Figgis, standing at the foot blocking her way, a puzzled expression creasing her face, brought her to an abrupt halt. 'What are you doing here? How did you get in?'

The voice of Rich Mallory's cleaner had

much the same instantly bracing effect as the proverbial cold shower. Allegedly. She'd never found the need for such self-abuse.

'Through the French windows, Mrs Figgis,' Ginny said, clinging to the truth. Her voice shocked back to crispness. Besides, having bearded the lion in his den and escaped in one piece, she wasn't about to be scared by someone wielding nothing more dangerous than a duster.

Nevertheless, she held her position two steps up. Just to even up the cleaner's height advantage.

A mistake. It just drew attention to her boots. Puzzlement instantly shifted to disapproval.

'Can I ask you to be careful when you're going round with a vacuum cleaner?' she asked. Getting it in before she was on the receiving end of a lecture about leaving footwear at the door—particularly anything as unsuitable as boots—in keeping with the Japanese theme of the décor. 'I'm afraid I've lost my hamster—'

'Hamster?'

What was it about hamsters that was so unbelievable?

All across the country people kept hamsters as pets. As an undergraduate, she'd briefly shared rooms with a girl who'd kept one. It had escaped all the time. It had even got under the floorboards once. Life with a hamster was a constant drama.

That was where she'd got the idea in the first place...

'Small, buff coloured rodent. About so big.' She sketched the rough dimensions with her hands. 'He's called Hector,' she said, her head distancing itself from her mouth as she elaborated unnecessarily. Or maybe not.

She probably thought a woman who kept a hamster as a pet would be a sad-sack obsessive—not true, her room-mate had been the life and soul of any party—but Richard Mallory would undoubtedly mention the incident, be suspicious if Mrs Figgis knew nothing about it. With good reason.

'Easy to mistake for fluff in a dark corner,' she added.

'There is no fluff in any corner of this apartment,' the woman declared indignantly.

'No, of course not. I didn't mean...' Then, 'I'm sure Mr Mallory will explain.'

'Mr Mallory?' Mrs Figgis blanched. 'He's still here?' So she wasn't the only one who'd been caught out. 'He should have left hours ago.'

'Really?' she said. Oh, listen to her to pretending not to know! She was shocked at just how convincing she sounded. 'Well, it's still early.' If you were a multi-millionaire businessman who'd just had a hard night with a girl who wore black silk stockings. 'Actually, I think he might appreciate coffee. And he did mention something about scrambled eggs...'

She didn't hang around to see whether Mrs Figgis considered it any part of her duties to make coffee rather than drink it. Instead, she headed swiftly in the direction of the French windows, legging it across the formerly immaculate raked gravel of Richard Mallory's roof garden before scrambling through Her Ladyship's now less than pristine hedge.

She didn't stop until she was safely inside, with her own French windows shut firmly against the outside world.

Only then did she lean back against them and let out a huge groan.

Rich Mallory straightened under the shower, letting the hot water ease the knots in his shoulders, the ache from the back of his neck. These all-night sessions took it out of him. They were a young man's game.

Then he grinned.

Okay, he was well past the downhill marker of thirty, but he could still teach the whizkids who worked for him a thing or two, even if he did need a massage to straighten out the kinks next morning.

Maybe he should have lived up—or was that down?—to his reputation and taken up the offer in Ginny Lautour's disturbing eyes. They were curiously at odds with her clothes, her mousy, not quite blonde hair caught back in a kid's scrunchy adorned with a velvet duck-billed platypus; he knew it was a duck-billed platypus because he'd been handbagged by his five-year-old niece into buying her one just like it.

But there was nothing childlike about her eyes. A curious mixture of grey and green and slightly slanted beneath finely marked brows, they were intense, witch's eyes...

His grin faded as he shook his head, flipped the jet to cold and stood beneath it while he counted slowly to twenty. Only then did he reach for his robe, towelling his hair as he padded back to his bedroom, trailing wet footprints across the pale carpet.

Orange juice. Coffee. Eggs. In that order. He'd been wise to pass on the side order of sex. Not that he hadn't been tempted. Beneath the shapeless clothes, Ginny Lautour's body had hinted at the kind of curves that invited a man's hand to linger. And her eyes had invited a lot more than that. But he wasn't ready to be bewitched just yet.

He'd beaten off several attempts to break through his security cordon, steal the latest software his company had developed which was now going through the rigorous testing phase. He'd hoped that they, whoever they were, had given up. Apparently not.

But he was smiling again as he picked up a phone, hitting the fast dial to his Chief Software Engineer as he headed downstairs in the direction of the kitchen. Despite the fact that she had been lying through her pretty teeth—not even the most athletic hamster could have got into that drawer—he'd enjoyed watching Ginny getting into deeper and deeper water as she had tried to extricate herself from an impossible situation.

For a girl in the industrial espionage

business she had a quite remarkable propensity to blush. It gave her a look of total innocence that was so completely at odds with the hot look in her eyes that a man might just be fooled into believing it.

Maybe he'd be a little less relaxed about it if there'd been anything of any value in his apartment for her to steal. As it was, he was rather looking forward to her next move.

'Marcus.' He jerked his mind back to more immediate concerns as his call was picked up. 'I've finally cracked the problem we've been having.'

Then, as the spiral turned inward so that he was facing into the vast expanse of his living room, he saw the open bottle of champagne standing on the sofa table and belatedly remembered the luscious redhead he'd taken to the retirement party he'd thrown for one of his senior staff.

'I'll be with you in half an hour to bring the team up to speed,' he said, not waiting for an answer before he disconnected.

Well, that explained the earring. It was Lilianne's. She must have taken him at his word when he had told her that he'd just be five minutes, invited her to make herself comfortable.

How long had she lain in his bed, waiting for him to join her? How long before she'd stormed out in a huff? Even he could see that it would have to be a huff. At the very least.

Long enough to write him a note and tie it to the neck of the champagne bottle with one of her stockings, anyway. Presumably to emphasize what he'd missed.

He sighed. She'd been playing kiss-chase with him for weeks and he'd be lying if he denied that he'd enjoyed the game. Hard to get was so rare these days. He wasn't fooled, of course. He understood the game too well for that. She believed the longer she held out, the greater would be her victory.

Not that he was objecting.

He'd been looking forward to the promised pay off. Which would have been last night if he hadn't suddenly caught a glimpse of the answer to a problem that had been giving his entire development team a headache for the last couple of weeks. He checked his wristwatch. The best part of ten hours ago.

He tugged at the stocking, caught a hint of the musky scent she'd been wearing. He really needed to concentrate on one thing at a time, he decided, as the napkin fell into the melted ice.

Work—nine-till-five. Personal life—

Forget it. Work was his life.

He shrugged, picked up the napkin. Her note was short and to the point.

LOSER.

Succinct. To the point. No wasted words. He admired brevity in a woman.

However, there was still the earring found by his uninvited caller. An earring not meant to be found by a casual glance. It suggested that she'd given herself a chance to call him—after sufficient time had elapsed for him to understand that she was seriously annoyed—and offer him the opportunity to tease her into forgiving him. Resume the chase.

And he grinned.

Then, as the scent of coffee brewing reached him, his eyes narrowed. It seemed as if Ginny Lautour hadn't been in as much of a hurry as she'd made out...

He left the note where it was and, tossing the stocking over the arm of the sofa, headed for the kitchen.

'So, you decided to stay for breakfast after all—'

He came to an abrupt halt as he realised

it was his cleaner—rather than his interesting new neighbour—who was making coffee. It left him with oddly mixed feelings.

Relief that she hadn't, after all, taken up his casual invitation to stick around, taking advantage of an unexpected opportunity to get close to him. That she hadn't been that obvious.

Disappointment...for much the same reason.

Not that he doubted she'd be back. Like the earring, Hector gave her all the excuse she needed to drop by any time she felt like it. Which was fine. He didn't believe for one minute that she was a criminal mastermind. He simply wanted to know who was pulling her strings.

'Good morning, Mr Mallory. I've made fresh coffee. Would you like me to cook breakfast for you?'

'No. Thank you, Mrs Figgis.' He'd lost his appetite. 'I'll have something at the office.' Then, 'You'll keep a look-out for Miss Lautour's hamster?'

'Of course. I'm sorry she disturbed you,' she said. 'If I'd realised you were home...'

'Late night. No problem.'

Far from it. If he'd left for the office at the usual time, or even taken this Friday off as he had originally planned and driven off into deepest Gloucestershire, Ginny Lautour could have searched his flat from top to bottom at her leisure and he doubted it would have crossed his cleaner's mind to even mention it.

The hamster, he realised, was a clever excuse. It was possible he'd underestimated the girl. No, that wasn't right, either. She might blush like a girl, but she had the eyes, the body of a woman...

'She's staying in the McBrides' apartment this summer?' he asked. It wouldn't hurt to double check.

'That's right. Keeping an eye on the place. She's a very quiet young lady,' she said. 'For a student.'

Maybe. Being quiet didn't preclude dishonesty. The prize of newly developed Mallory software was enough to tempt the most innocent of souls. Or maybe she was doing it for some man.

She might blush like a nineteenth-century village maiden, but those eyes didn't belong to a nice quiet girl.

'She's a student?'

'According to Lady McBride's daily.'

'And she's living there on her own?'

'Yes. She wants some peace and quiet to work, apparently.'

'I see. Well, let me know if you find the creature.'

'Yes, Mr Mallory.'

He poured himself coffee, calling his secretary as he retreated to his bedroom.

'Wendy,' he said, as she picked up the phone. 'I need you to organise some flowers.'

'For the lovely Lilianne?' she asked, hopefully.

'No.' She'd forfeited the flowers and the apology when she'd indulged herself with that cryptic note.

For that he'd make her sweat a bit before he called her again.

'What happened?' Wendy demanded, interrupting his train of thought.

'What? Oh, nothing happened.'

'Nothing? You left the party with the most beautiful woman in the room in one hand and a bottle of champagne in the other. What went wrong?'

'Not a thing. I just had an idea, that's all. I didn't think it would take more than five minutes to check it out—'

'And before you noticed, it was morning. You are the absolute limit, Richard.'

'I'm a total loss as a human being,' he agreed. 'But my computer loves me.'

'A computer won't keep you warm in your old age.'

'No, but it'll pay the electricity company to do the job.'

'You'll end up a lonely old bachelor,' she warned.

'Read the gossip columns, Wendy,' he said, rapidly growing bored with this conversation. 'There are no lonely old millionaires. Bachelor or otherwise.' Then, 'The flowers are for my sister. It's her wedding anniversary.'

'I've already ordered some.'

'Have you? When?'

'The moment the invitation arrived. I offered to have a little bet with the girls in the office on the likelihood of you wriggling out of a long weekend of come-and-join-us marital bliss. Your sister, bless her, isn't subtle. She wants you married and producing cousins for her own offspring while there's a chance they'll be in the same generation. But they all know you too well. I had no takers. Not even the new girl in the software lab.'

She was kidding. She had to be kidding...

'Save the smug gloating for the ladies room, Wendy, and sort out a working lunch for the research and development team in the boardroom for one o'clock. I'll be there in thirty minutes—'

'I really think you should send Lilianne flowers too,' she said, not in the least bothered by his Chairman of the Board act. 'At the very least.'

Wendy had been with him since he'd started the company and had seen him through the bad times as well as the good. She thought it gave her the right to treat him like a rather bossy nanny. Occasionally, he allowed her to get away with it. But not today.

'I really don't have the time for this—'

'Is the situation salvageable, do you think? What kind of statement do you want to make?'

Who did he think he was kidding? She always got away with it.

'No statement of any kind.' But, since he recognised a brick wall when he saw one, and he'd meant it when he had said he hadn't got time for petty details, he went on, 'Okay, I'll concede on the flowers.' And honesty compelled him to admit that Lilianne had had a point. She did deserve an apology. 'But they are not to be red roses. Not roses of any hue.'

'Terribly vulgar, red roses,' she agreed. 'And, besides, you're right. It would be unkind to raise any serious expectations in the lady's breast. She is, after all, just another passing fancy.'

'And what the devil is that supposed to mean?'

'Only that she's out of the same mould as every girl you've ever dated. Only the names—and hair colour—change.' About to protest, he realised it would be quicker to just let her get on with it. 'But you're like all men; you see the pretty wrapping and you're hooked. Temporarily. Of course, the clever women realise very quickly that they're always going to be playing second fiddle to your computer and throw you back—'

Okay, that was it. 'Is this conversation going somewhere?'

She sighed. 'Obviously not. Leave it with me. I'll sort out something that will put her in a forgiving mood. Anything else?'

'No. Yes. Have you ever kept a hamster?'

'A hamster is not a substitute for a

proper relationship,' she replied sternly. 'But I suppose it's a marginal improvement on a computer. Why?'

'I'm informed there's one on the loose in my apartment.'

'Then guard your cables. My kids had one and, I promise you, they can chew through anything.'

'Oh, great. Better make that an hour while I make sure that at least my study is a hamster free zone.'

He might not be totally convinced about the hamster, but he wasn't prepared to take any chances.

Miss Iphegenia Lautour might have a ridiculous propensity to blush for a grown woman. He wasn't, however, about to overlook the possibility that she could have let loose a small furry friend in order to provide herself with a legitimate excuse for searching his apartment.

Why pretend when you could do it for real?

An answer immediately offered itself. Why would she complicate things with livestock?

A real hamster would, sooner or later, be found. Maybe too soon. An imaginary one, on the other hand, would provide her with endless opportunities to return.

Just how clever was she? The image might be pure innocence, but the eyes had glowed with something that had warned him not to take any chances.

He'd be well-advised, he decided, not to take anything for granted, but to assume the worst.

Ginny, too agitated to be able to concentrate, didn't make it to the Underground station before she abandoned all thoughts of work. Instead, she bought a sandwich and a carton of coffee and retired to a small park where she tossed crumbs to the sparrows, putting off the evil moment when she'd have to call Sophie and let her know that she'd failed.

But eventually she ran out of sandwiches and time.

She dug out her cellphone, keyed in the number. Her call was answered with an alacrity that suggested Sophie had been sitting with the phone in her hand.

'What happened?' she demanded without preamble.

There was no soft answer. 'I'm sorry, Sophie, but his desk was locked. I tried to find a key but when I went upstairs...' She hesitated. Did she want to entertain Sophie with her encounter with Richard Mallory? Definitely not. 'I was interrupted.'

'Interrupted? Who by?' she demanded.

'It's fine, Sophie. No problem.'

'Oh.' For a moment Ginny had the feeling that she was disappointed. 'Well, that's good, isn't it? You can have another try tomorrow.'

No! 'Look, why don't you just own up? Surely Richard Mallory will understand? You can't be the first person ever to delete a file.'

'You don't understand! I should have backed it up! I should have made copies! I should—'

'Sophie! Pull yourself together!' Heavens, she'd never been in this kind of state about a job before. She must be really desperate to keep it. 'It has to be in the system somewhere. Can't you flutter your eyelashes at one of those clever young men who work for him?'

'No! This is a serious job and I want to keep it. I can't admit to messing up. Besides, it's not that easy. Go poking around in the memory of the mainframe and alarms get triggered off. The man is paranoid about security.'

'Well, thank you for telling me that,' Ginny said drily.

'What? Oh...' Then she laughed. 'Oh, I see what you mean. You're safe enough in his apartment. He wouldn't expect anyone to break in there, would he? And it's not as if it's his precious secret development stuff you're after.'

'But would he believe that?'

'He's never going to know. I've told you, it's his sister's wedding anniversary and he's playing happy families in Gloucestershire.'

Maybe that's where he should have been, but he'd clearly been distracted by a pair of silk clad legs...

'Listen to me, Ginny. It is absolutely vital that you get that disk. I have to prove to my father that I can keep a job.'

'Why?'

There was a pause, then a sigh, then Sophie said, 'He's had enough of subsidising me, that's why.'

Something she'd never have to worry about, Ginny thought. But what she'd never had, she'd never miss. 'Hasn't he threatened to cut you off without so much as a brass farthing at least half a dozen times since you left home? You know he doesn't mean it.'

'He does *this* time and it's all my sister's fault,' Sophie added.

'What's Kate done to deserve the blame?'

'She got married. To a wealthy barrister. A man who will, in the fullness of time, inherit a title and a country estate. It's put ideas into Daddy's head. He's compared the cost of a wedding against the cost of supporting me and decided a wedding makes more economic sense in the long term. He's actually got some chinless wonder lined up and panting to take me off his hands.'

'Does he have a title and country estate to look forward to?'

'Does it matter if he hasn't got a chin? I have three choices, Ginny. Marry him. Marry someone else. Or support myself.'

'Tough choice,' Ginny said.

But Sophie didn't get sarcasm. 'The worst!' she exclaimed. 'All that's saving me from a fate worse than death is this job...'

'He might not be a chinless wonder, Sophie. He might be, well, jolly nice.'

'Of course he'll be "nice". I don't want "nice", I want...' She stopped abruptly. 'I mean, really, Ginny, would you marry someone your father had picked out for you?' Then, 'Oh, damn! I'm sorry...I didn't mean...'

Oh, rats! Now Sophie felt guilty.

'It's okay,' Ginny said quickly. 'Don't fret.'

Despite the fact that they were total opposites in just about every respect, they'd bonded on their first day at school. It had been Sophie who, as the social queen of the class, had saved her from the fallout of being given the kind of name that no five-year-old should be saddled with.

As the solitary child of a feminist scholar—dismissive of playgroups and nursery schools—Ginny had little experience of mixing with children of her own age. She hadn't realised that her name *was* odd until she ran into the cruel ridicule of the classroom.

Sophie had recognised a born outsider and, for some reason neither of them had ever quite fathomed, had taken her under her wing. Maybe it was the attraction of opposites. She hadn't questioned it at the time, too grateful that since everyone wanted to be part of Sophie's charmed circle the teasing had instantly stopped.

While her odd background, a lack of interest in the latest fashion, boys or parties and an inclination for solitary study had meant that she'd never actually been part of the group, she'd never been an outsider after that, at least not at school.

And once out in the big wide world she'd quickly learned to deal with the rest of the world in her own way.

'Look, don't worry. I'll have another go, okay?'

'Will you? Thank goodness Philly talked her in-laws into letting you ''sit'' their apartment for the summer. I just wish you could have had my spare room. Only Aunt Cora has saddled me with visitors for the summer.'

'It is her apartment, Sophie.' And, much as she loved Sophie, she was in London to work. She'd get a lot more of that done in the quiet of the McBrides' apartment.

'I suppose. And jolly lucky in the circumstances.'

That, Ginny thought, rather depended upon your point of view.

But it would be okay, she reassured herself. By now Mallory would have left for his delayed weekend in the country. All she had to do was get past Mrs Figgis and her duster. Which actually might not be that difficult...

'Hector,' she said, as she dropped her cellphone into her bag. 'You're back on.'

'Richard?'

Richard Mallory looked up from the pad on which he'd been doodling a hamster. Wearing outsize spectacles. A slightly dishevelled hamster with a twig dangling over one ear and her cheeks aflame...

It suddenly occurred to him that everyone was waiting for him to say something.

He did a fast mental rewind, then, getting to his feet, he said, 'We're pushing a deadline here. I want this done today.'

Wendy, who'd been sitting beside him taking notes, followed him into his office, shutting the door behind her.

'So,' she said, holding up the notepad he'd left on the boardroom table. 'Tell me about the hamster.'

'*Mesocricetus Auratus Auratus.*' He'd taken the time to look it up. 'The golden hamster is a small nocturnal mammal discovered in the Syrian desert in the early twentieth century. Very popular as a children's pet although, since it's only awake during the hours of darkness, I don't see the attraction—'

'Believe me, if you were the small pet of a curious child you'd choose to be nocturnal.' Then, 'Okay, ten out of ten for doing your homework. Now, tell me about the one with the cute spectacles. Is that a blush?'

He took the pad from her, looked at the drawing for a moment, his body responding uncomfortably to the memory of the delicate pink flush that had heated Ginny Lautour's cheeks, the silky touch of her hair as he'd untangled a piece of shrubbery. A pair of grey-green eyes that had lit up from inside, overriding the 'ignore me' effect of unflattering clothes.

'She's apartment-sitting for my next-door neighbour,' he said, tossing it on his desk behind him. Where he couldn't see it.

'Excuse me? Are you telling me that she's a real, old-fashioned, honest to goodness girl next door?'

'She's real enough. And she lives next door.'

Further than that, he was not prepared to commit himself.

Wendy retrieved the notepad and took

another look. 'I want to know everything. What's her name?'

He didn't immediately answer. His mind was too busy struggling with the image of her lower lip, full and luscious. The tip of her tongue cooling it…

Had it been an unconscious response to something that had crackled in the air between them? Or deliberate. A practised attempt to entice…

'Trouble,' he said abruptly.

Just how much trouble he'd know once he'd got the results of the security checks he was running on her.

CHAPTER THREE

GINNY rang Richard Mallory's doorbell.

She'd checked the basement car park—
something that she'd have been well advised to do before she'd blundered in earlier—and his parking space was now
empty. He'd finally left for his weekend in
the country and the coast was clear.

Nevertheless, she'd be kidding herself if
she pretended that her heart was beating at
anything like a normal tempo. That her
hands weren't horribly clammy. That she
was feeling anything like as cool as she
hoped she looked...

'Oh, Miss Lautour.' In an effort to impress Mrs Figgis, Ginny had changed from
her boots, jeans and her purple shirt and
was now wearing the kind of shoes that
wouldn't harm the blond flooring, a long
feminine skirt with a tank top and an expensive white linen shirt that hung to her
thighs. The woman still didn't look partic-

ularly pleased to see her. 'Have you found your…pet?'

Her expression suggested that she did not have a very high opinion of young women who kept small furry creatures as pets. Worse. Allowed them to escape into other people's apartments.

'I'm afraid not. Which is why, since I realise how much extra work he's going to cause you until he's found, I hope you'll accept this.'

She offered the woman an apologetic smile—it wasn't difficult, she was very sorry she was doing this. Deeply sorry. But she couldn't abandon Sophie in her hour of need. Besides, she would gain a great deal of satisfaction from outwitting Richard Mallory. Once it was over and done with and she could enjoy her triumph in the quiet of her own living room.

'A small apology in advance.'

And she handed over the carrier she was holding.

'Work?' Mrs Figgis was distracted by the exotically flowering pot plant trailing out of the bag.

'Cleaning up after him. He'll tear up paper—' she gave a little shrug '—well, anything really to make a nest. And he'll leave, well, mess. Especially since he'll be frightened. I feel really bad about that and I just wanted to say that you must call me to deal with it.'

'Mess?' Mrs Figgis looked up, finally catching on to what Ginny was saying. 'You mean he'll leave droppings everywhere? Like a mouse?' Her face was a picture of outrage at the very idea.

'Pretty much,' she said. She'd never been allowed to keep any kind of pet, but one small rodent's droppings would be much like another, surely? And then, crossing her fingers behind her back, 'I just hope he doesn't chew through Mr Mallory's beautiful carpets.'

That did it. Mrs Figgis opened the door wide to admit her. 'Why don't you come in and have a thorough look round? Now. Before he can do any damage.'

Yes!

'Won't it hold you up? You must be leaving soon. I can always come back later,' she offered. 'When Mr Mallory's at home.'

'He's a busy man. I don't think we need to bother him with this again.' Two women but with a single thought… 'I've got some ironing I can be getting on with.'

'If you're sure?' It really had been too much to hope that Mallory's 'daily' would leave her to get on with her search unsupervised, with nothing more than a reminder to set the alarm before she left. She stepped inside. 'This is really kind of you. I'll be as quick as I can.'

'Take your time, Miss Lautour. I'll go home a lot happier if I know there's nothing running around in here leaving messes.' And she shuddered.

Now Ginny felt *really* guilty. She'd think of some way to make it up to the woman. Get her tickets for some West End show, perhaps? Maybe she could take the porter…

Her conscience partially salved by this opportunity to encourage the course of true love, she followed Mrs Figgis into the huge double storey living room where all trace of Rich Mallory's dalliance with the wearer of black silk stockings had been cleaned and polished away.

'Why don't you start upstairs, Miss Lautour? Work your way down.'

'What? Oh, right.' She looked at the spiral staircase. Going back up there was the last thing in the world she wanted to do, she discovered. But there was no putting it off. Keys to find. Sophie's hide to save. 'Good idea,' she said, putting on a bright smile.

Actually, she thought it was probably the worst idea she'd ever heard.

He's not there, she reminded herself. He wasn't zonked out under the bedclothes after a night of passion. He was on his way to Gloucestershire. Presumably to try out the passion in a different bed.

Forget him!

She opened the door to his bedroom. It was now flooded with sunlight and the covers lay smooth on the vast bed with not so much as a speck of dust to disturb the lacquered finish of his bedside tables. Yet his presence was as strong as if he was in the room with her.

As if he was pinning her back against the door, the exciting scent of his skin doing unimaginable things to her inside.

She took a deep breath.

Nonsense.

Her nerves were on edge, that was all. They had every right to be on edge; she was putting them through the kind of experience that nerves could well do without.

And the sooner she got on with this, the sooner they would be able to relax. She quickly dealt with the drawer she'd missed earlier. An old wallet. Photographs of his family... What looked like recent holiday pictures of a young woman, enough like him to be his sister, with two young children. There was just one old picture. It was of Mallory himself at that gangling adolescent stage when hands and feet didn't fit the rest of him; he had an arm thrown about the neck of an equally uncoordinated mongrel pup.

She found herself battling with a lump in her throat. A man who kept a picture of his dog couldn't be a total monster, could he?

She swallowed hard. It didn't matter what he was, she told herself as she replaced the pictures and moved on to the bathroom. It had nothing to do with her. All she wanted was that disk.

As if anyone in their right mind would keep a spare key in the bathroom, she told herself as she went through the cupboards. It did give her the opportunity to check out his aftershave, though. She approved...

What was she doing? Lingering over nonsense when she should be in his dressing room. If there was a key, that was where it would be.

The cufflink drawers contained nothing but cufflinks. Dozens of pairs of cufflinks. Birthday…Christmas presents. Well, what else did a girl—girls—give a man who had everything?

She opened another drawer and had her answer. Ties. Pure silk, designer label ties. Every one of them with a touch of the same perfect blue as his eyes…

The remaining drawers contained nothing more exciting than neatly folded socks, beautifully ironed shirts, underwear. Her fingers lingered over a pair of soft grey shorts and she found her mind drifting back to the sight of him that morning. Exciting enough…

She snatched back her hand, slammed the drawer shut and, turning to the wardrobes that lined the opposite wall, began to work her way swiftly through the pockets of his clothes. But in her heart of hearts she knew it was pointless. Mrs Figgis was not a woman to hang up a jacket without first emptying the pockets.

She heard the bedroom door open behind her as Mrs Figgis came to hurry her along and she dived into the bottom of the wardrobe.

'Hector,' she cooed, picking up a hard

worn walking boot and sticking her hand inside. 'Where are you, sweetheart...?' As her fingers encountered something soft and hairy she dropped it with a nervous shriek, backing swiftly out of the wardrobe. She'd thought her heart was beating fast... *Now* it was beating fast...

She swallowed, pulled herself together and picked up the boot to get a better look.

'It's a sock,' she said, and laughed with relief. 'Just an old woollen sock.' Not even Mrs Figgis was one hundred per cent perfect. She looked up, expecting to see her standing in the doorway with that disapproving look curling her upper lip.

'Drat' did not seem nearly strong enough to express her feelings as she discovered that it wasn't the housekeeper but Rich Mallory watching her with an expression that she couldn't begin to fathom. But he wasn't smiling.

'This is the second time I've found you in my bedroom. Are you trying to tell me something?' He spoke with the cool assurance of a man who'd been fending off eager women since puberty. Clearly convinced that this was simply another case of a pathetic woman flinging herself at him.

She *knew* he'd never believed in Hector…

Ginny, inwardly seething at being forced into such a position, swallowed her pride, dredged up a smile from the very depths of her soul and said, 'It looks bad, doesn't it?'

'The gossip columnists would have a field day,' he agreed. 'But if you don't tell them, I won't.'

He reached out a hand to help her to her feet.

Since her legs seemed incapable of managing this simple act for themselves, she took it. His fingers wrapped about her hand and for a moment neither of them moved. For a moment everything was so still that it felt as if time itself had stopped.

Then he pulled her up and, since he didn't step back, her nose finished up uncomfortably close to his shirt front. The scent of soft linen overlaying warm skin.

Not for the first time, she wished she was taller. Except then it would have been his throat, or his chin, or his mouth that she would have been no more than a breath away from.

She made a determined effort to look up. Say something intelligent…

'At least you're dressed this time.'

And looking totally fantastic in a cream linen suit and a band collar dark blue shirt.

'Stick around,' he offered.

'No need.' He was still clasping her hand, holding it against his chest so that she could feel the slow, steady thud of his heartbeat. 'I already know your taste in underwear.'

Oh, brilliant, Ginny! Why don't you just say what you're thinking…?

She cleared her throat. 'Actually, I'm here because Mrs Figgis wanted me to—'

'I know. She explained. You've had no luck yet?' And once again Ginny had the disconcerting feeling that he wasn't talking about Hector.

'Um…'

His detached expression finally softened, the tiniest contraction of the lines fanning out from his eyes, his mouth widening into a slow, wide, oddly provoking smile that for a moment held her his captive. Then she snatched her hand away, as if by breaking the connection she could somehow get her brain back in gear.

She used it to push her spectacles up her nose.

Rich forgot all about the fact that Ginny Lautour was ransacking his wardrobe looking for a spare key to his desk and instead found himself wondering what she'd do with her hands if she didn't have her spectacles as a prop. If she didn't have them to hide behind. And what were they hiding?

There was only one way to find out.

He removed them—ignoring her gasp of outrage—and held them up out of her reach, checking them against the light, reassuring himself that they weren't just that—a prop, a disguise.

They were real enough, he discovered. The lady was, apparently, a touch short-sighted. But he wasn't surrendering them too soon. Instead, he opened a drawer, took out a clean handkerchief and began to polish them.

Her fingers twitched as if it was all she could do to stop herself from grabbing them back. He finished one lens, moved on to the next, taking his time about it so that he could get a good look at her eyes.

He hadn't been mistaken about them. Grey and green intermingled in a bewitching combination beneath a curtain of dark lashes that were all hers. No magic mascara to lengthen or curl them, they'd be soft to the touch, silk to his lips, he thought. And he wanted to touch.

Like Ginny, he restrained himself. For the moment. He continued to polish the lens. Here, in the artificial light of his dressing room, the silver-grey was dominant. But beneath the silver the green was shimmering dangerously.

He'd caught a glimpse of it that morning—a flash of recklessness, heat quickly damped down. Like the glimpse of curves offered by the clinging top she was wearing beneath the loose enfolding shirt, it had lingered with him, far more enticing than the most revealing gown.

More exciting than the most blatant of invitations, this veiled promise of hidden fire tugged at something deep inside him.

Or was it simply a mask to hide her true purpose? Hidden away beneath clothes chosen to conceal, behind the large spectacles, who was the real Ginny Lautour?

The name was uncommon. And yet familiar.

He would find out.

He took one final look at the spectacles. 'They were dusty,' he said, sliding them back into place. But as his thumbs brushed against the hot flush of her cheek, his fingers tangled with the silky hair that trailed over her ears, he'd have been hard pressed to say which of them was trembling. And with her face turned up her lips seemed to offer him the kind of temptation only a saint could be expected to refuse.

Well, he might not be quite such a sinner as his reputation implied, but any woman who strayed into his bedroom—twice— could hardly expect to escape without paying a penalty. And he lowered his lips to hers.

Soft, sweet, warm.

The heat was building fast and for a moment his palms cupped her cheeks, his fingers sliding through her hair and holding her his captive.

Not that she was offering any kind of resistance. No shocked outrage, the slap he almost certainly deserved. On the contrary, her mouth was clinging to his, her whole body softening against him in a seductive ambush that whispered enchantment in his ear. Stirring not just his body but his soul.

He lifted his head, easing back mere inches so that he could look at her, read her eyes. For a moment she did not move, but remained perfectly still as if moving would break some spell. Then she gave a little sigh and opened her eyes.

They were a clear, translucent green.

Yes! He knew it! He'd sensed the ambiguities in this woman's character, a secret core that she allowed no one to see. And he'd tapped right into it.

For a moment he felt exultant. As if he'd found the gold at the end of a rainbow. Captured the essence of this woman with a single kiss.

Then reality rushed back.

Could it be that he was the one who'd just been captured?

That her imperfect disguise had been deliberate. That he'd been meant to see through it.

Or was he, perhaps, losing his mind?

'It's not true, you know,' he said.

Her mouth moved as she tried to say something but no sound emerged. She cleared her throat and tried again. 'What?'

'They're no protection. Men do make passes at girls who wear glasses. Think about that next time you're tempted to spend any time in my bedroom.' Then, because it occurred to him that might be construed as an invitation, he let go of her, took a step back, putting clear air between them.

Ginny was floundering.

She should not have come back. The

warning had been there when he'd touched her cheek before, in the unexpected yearning for him to touch her again, more intimately. In the way her body had delayed her even when her brain was telling her to get out of there while the going was good.

Now Richard Mallory had kissed her and it was as if her entire history was wiped clean. She had completely forgotten her determination to stay clear of involvement at all costs, knowing that her name brought with it baggage that she could never live down.

All it had taken was one little kiss to trigger off an emotional chain reaction that had her heading towards meltdown.

Well, *hello*, fool!

The urgent heat of desire was followed by an even swifter anger. She wanted to tell him exactly what she thought of him, that he should keep his hands to himself. Her brain warned her to keep quiet. That it was always better to keep quiet. It was a near run thing but the brain won.

That had never let her down.

But how had he known? About the glasses?

'Have you finished in here?' he asked

abruptly. 'Checked all my shoes? Been through all the drawers?'

'Yes,' she said quickly, taking a step back herself, putting herself out of his reach in case he could read her mind. She really hoped he couldn't read her mind... 'No!'

'Well, that was decisive.' It came out more harshly than Rich had intended. He didn't want to scare her away. He still needed to know all her secrets. He just wasn't prepared to share his.

'You startled me. I didn't expect... Mrs Figgis said you were going away. This morning...'

So that was why she was back. She'd thought he'd gone. But what on earth did she expect to find in his shoes? He doubted that she was looking for his old socks.

'There was a change of plan. Maybe tomorrow,' he said, cruelly holding out hope that she might yet find herself with time and opportunity to search his apartment. Then, 'I do hope you went through everything.' It wasn't as if there was anything for her to find. He'd cleared out anything in the least bit useful to a competitor. Left only a baited hook. With an invisible line attached. 'I'd really hate to come back and discover that Hector had taken up residence—' he glanced pointedly at the sock she was still holding on to as if her very life depended upon it '—in my sock drawer.'

'He's not in here,' she said, dropping it on the dressing table as if scalded. 'I'd better go—'

'No.' He reached out and caught her wrist as she made a move to pass him. 'Please carry on with what you're doing,' he demanded. 'Ignore me. Forget I'm here.'

'Easier said than done,' she declared, her chest rising and falling rapidly beneath the clinging top she was wearing under a long unbuttoned shirt. He made a determined effort to ignore it. 'You have a way of making your presence felt.'

'It's my apartment. And you invited yourself in.'

'Mrs Figgis invited me in,' she declared roundly.

'Did she have any choice?' No answer. 'If you want to look around, I suggest you get on with it. But, if you've finished in here, I'd like to change.'

He released her wrist, peeled off his jacket, tossed it aside. Carefully emptied his trouser pockets, tossing his wallet and keys on to the dressing table. Then began on the buttons of his shirt. He was tugging it out of his trousers when he realised that they were still standing eyeball to eyeball. That she hadn't moved a muscle.

'You're welcome to stay and watch,' he offered. 'But, as you've already reminded me, you won't be seeing anything new.'

Sophie was right, Ginny decided. The man was a bastard. She had started to check the lower levels of the bookshelves—just for show—while she tried to work out how she was going to use this unexpected turn of events to her advantage.

Rich Mallory turning up might have been her worst nightmare… But, despite the fact that he'd kissed her witless, it was not a total disaster. The taste of his mouth might be clinging to her lips, the flash of heat still burning in her veins, but just yards away from her his keys were lying on his dressing table.

All she had to do was get back into there and, well, if Bob wasn't exactly going to be her uncle, he was certainly going to be a second cousin.

Right at that moment she didn't know how she was going to manage it, but she did know that she wasn't giving up, because this was no longer just about saving Sophie's job.

It was personal.

It took a special kind of arrogance to assume that a woman only had to look at him for her to immediately want to fall into bed with him.

Even if it was probably true. She certainly hadn't done anything to disabuse him.

She stopped her angry poking at the bookshelves, lowered her head and banged it against the shelves.

He wasn't the only one who'd behaved badly. She hadn't exactly turned on the outrage, had she? Hadn't demanded to know what the devil he thought he was doing. Slapped his face.

She hadn't even stepped back, made it clear that she wasn't interested. He was the one who'd cut the connection.

She'd just let him kiss her. More than let him. She'd co-operated. Enthusiastically. It wasn't just Richard Mallory she was angry with. She was equally at fault. After all, he was just living down to his reputation and she should have expected nothing better from him.

Well, maybe she was a bit surprised that he'd bother to flirt with someone like her. It wasn't as if she dressed provocatively or did anything to encourage flirtation. Quite the opposite.

And she didn't even own a pair of black silk stockings.

She got to her feet. Maybe it was the novelty of kissing someone who wasn't wearing lipstick that had tempted him. That had to be a whole new sensory experience for him.

She touched her upper lip with the tip of her tongue, tasting him. It had certainly been a new experience for her...

She snapped back to reality. Who was she kidding?

She knew exactly what it was.

Poor girl, she looks like hell, probably hasn't had a pass made in her direction for so long she must be panting for it. He thought he was doing her a favour. Saw it as charity work.

Well, too bad. He was not as original as he thought.

Not that she cared one jot what he thought of her.

All she cared about was finding that disk and saving Sophie's job. And she was going to look him in the face and smile while she did it, no matter how hard that would be.

The fact that he would never know what she'd done, would always think of her as a slightly batty creature with a juvenile taste in pets, would make her victory all the sweeter.

She tried on the smile, just to practice, and she was still wearing it when Mallory appeared in the doorway. He'd changed into a pair of jeans and a t-shirt and it didn't take an airport X-ray machine for her to see that he wasn't carrying anything in his pockets. And her smile became the real article.

If he was surprised to find her grinning like an idiot he made no comment.

'Any luck?' he asked, as if he'd been hoping she'd have made herself scarce.

Tough. He'd scared her off once, but no one had ever accused her of not learning from her mistakes.

'Not yet, but then you never actually believed he could manage your spiral staircase, did you?'

'You're the expert,' he said, heading straight for it. 'I'm making coffee. Would you like a cup?'

'Thank you. Coffee would be very welcome.'

'Come on down, then.' He glanced back at her, paused. 'That's if you've finished up here? Or could you do with some help to look on the higher shelves?'

No! 'No, thanks.' She mentally urged him down the stairs. He didn't move. 'I've just about run out of places to look, to be honest.' Then she glanced around.

'Lost something?'

She nudged her bag behind the nearest chair with her foot. 'My bag. I must have left it in your, um…'

'Bedroom?'

'Mmm.'

There was a long pause. Then, a touch irritably he said, 'Well, what are you waiting for? Go and get it. I'll wait for you.'

She didn't want to appear too eager. 'I wouldn't want there to be any misunderstandings.'

'Do you want me to get it for you?'

'No, I'll fetch it. Just—stay here. Okay?'

He shrugged and she made herself take her time, a prickle at her neck warning her that he was watching her. Wanting to turn around and check, but that would have looked so guilty. Or worse. A come-on…

Once out of sight, however, she dashed into his dressing room, snatched up his keys. He wasn't watching her, of course. He couldn't see her from where he'd been standing. He'd probably gone straight down to the kitchen. Please...

When she emerged—still minus her bag—she discovered that he hadn't gone anywhere. He hadn't moved from the top of the stairs. He'd actually meant it when he'd said he'd wait.

Wretch.

'Oh, there it is!' she exclaimed like an idiot, picking it up from behind the chair. 'I'll lose my head one of these days...' Well, he already thought she was stupid. He could be right...

'All you appear to be missing now is one small rodent,' he said, his face expressionless. 'Why don't you take a look around the kitchen while I get the coffee.'

'You really think he'd have survived a whole day in the kitchen with Mrs Figgis?'

Where was Mrs Figgis, anyway?

'She's gone now. He's quite safe.'

'Oh.' Then, because that sounded as if being alone with him bothered her, 'I was admiring it earlier. Your kitchen.' She made a vague gesture that suggested the brushed steel rack above the central island. 'The, um, utensils.'

'Well, that's what they're for. Show. The finest, um, utensils an interior designer could find.'

She ignored this attempt at teasing her. She knew where that led. 'You don't cook?' she asked.

'Not unless I absolutely have to.'

'Pathetic.'

'Women are such critics. You're a gourmet cook, I suppose.' He stood back so that she could precede him into the kitchen. 'A domestic goddess.'

'Perish the thought. Life's too short for stuffing mushrooms—'

'Is it? I'm of the view that one should do most things once. I've been saving that one up for a rainy day.'

'But unlike men—' she pressed on, refusing to play '—most men, anyway, women do have to make the effort if they want to eat. Let's face it, no man is going to do it for them.'

'That, if I may say so, is a highly sexist remark. Any time you want a fried egg sandwich, just say the word.'

'And which word would that be?'

'You get three guesses.'

'And if I don't guess right?'

'You have to cook one for me.'

It wasn't fair—he shouldn't be able to make her laugh. Fortunately, he turned abruptly to the sink and filled the kettle.

'Don't mind me,' he said. 'Help yourself.'

While she toured the kitchen he took coffee beans from the state-of-the-art stainless steel American fridge.

She opened doors, making a pretence of looking for Hector, enjoying the chance to nose through his immaculate range of cookware, china, every kind of labour-saving electrical gadget a busy cook might dream of.

The only sound was of beans grinding.

She carried on looking. He had a food mixer that made her drool with envy. Maybe he'd let her borrow it. Just to test whether it actually worked.

No. Get the disk. Get out of there. Never return.

The silence lengthened. She knew he was watching her as he waited for the kettle. She moved a couple of boxes, thinking hard.

Now she had his keys, how on earth was

she going to distract him long enough to get into his study? Go through his desk?

Opening the door to the cupboard beneath the sink, she was confronted with the answer to her prayers.

'Oh, good grief,' she said. She hadn't had to work on sounding surprised. How often did you get that kind of divine intervention?

CHAPTER FOUR

'PROBLEM?' Mallory asked.

Ginny knelt down, poking her head right inside the cupboard to get a better look and taking her time about replying.

'Maybe.' His silence assured her that she had his full attention. Only then did she back out, look up and say, 'You don't suppose he could have squeezed down through there, do you?'

Rich paused. Having watched her performance as she toured the kitchen, he'd awaited her next move with interest. He'd say one thing for Ginny Lautour, she never disappointed.

'Where?' he asked.

'There's this hole…'

'Hole?' Suddenly she had his full attention.

'Well, not so much a hole as a gap…'

He took a deep breath, carefully finished spooning the coffee into the cafetière, poured on hot water and covered it before he folded himself up beside Ginny. Her shoulder nudged distractingly against his as she turned.

'Show me,' he said.

She pointed wordlessly to where the pipe from the sink to the waste outlet disappeared through the floor of the cupboard and he leaned closer to get a better look, doing his best to ignore her hair brushing against his face.

Between the pipe and the wall was a space big enough for the tubbiest of rodents to have squeezed down.

It was what rodents did, after all. They lived down holes.

What he couldn't see was what she hoped to gain by having him rip his kitchen apart looking for this imaginary friend. Unless, of course, she'd been telling the truth all along and he was just a sad cynic who always assumed an ulterior motive.

Glancing sideways at Ginny, at the soft curve of her lips that had quickened so enticingly beneath his, he discovered that he wanted, more than anything, to believe her.

Even when he knew she was deceiving him, when he tried to keep a distance between them, he still found himself responding to her. Grinning like some big kid who had just discovered that girls are not just a pain in the butt.

Suckered by a single innocent kiss.

Innocent? Who was he trying to kid? His thoughts had been a long way from innocent. As for hers...

He turned back to the cupboard and reality. 'Please tell me,' he said, 'that you're winding me up. That you don't seriously believe Hector might be down there?'

Ginny knew that she shouldn't do this. Her conscience was waving red flags, warning her that this was a seriously bad thing to do. As if she didn't know that already.

But what about him? He'd kissed her. Not because she was some willowy beauty that he was seriously lusting after, had wooed with dinner in some expensive restaurant, plied with champagne. Two equals playing the same game. No. He'd done it because he thought he was irresistible. Because it pleased his male ego to prove it.

Bad enough. But then, when she'd responded with more enthusiasm than sense—and surely if a man kissed a girl he hoped for that reaction?—he'd backed off faster than a rabbit confronted by a fox.

Even short, seriously unwillowy girls

merited a little more consideration than that. Not a quick step backwards and a don't-call-me-I'll-call-you about turn.

He deserved some pain.

And she needed a distraction. Something that would keep him occupied for long enough for her to save Sophie's bacon and get out of there.

So, although she knew her conscience would give her a hard time later, she crossed her fingers before looking straight into his dangerous blue eyes and before she could lose her nerve she said, 'Hector once got beneath the floorboards.'

'Here?'

'No, no. Not *here*. There are no loose floorboards in the McBrides' apartment.' His eyebrows invited—demanded—that she elaborate. 'It was in college,' she said.

This *had* actually happened, although not to her. Or Hector. Who Did Not Exist, she reminded herself. Her imaginary rodent was beginning to take on the heroic proportions of his namesake. She just hoped that Rich Mallory wouldn't prove to be his—or her—Achilles.

'They're old,' she explained. 'The college buildings. Gaps everywhere. The porters spent all day lifting them—the floor-boards—before he was finally cornered.'

Rich Mallory stared at her for a moment, his expression warring between horror and disbelief.

Then he said one brief word that clearly expressed everything he was feeling before he swept the contents of the cupboard to one side to take a closer look.

'Now what?' Ginny asked, as Mallory regarded the smooth white floor of the cup-board.

'Now I think I need someone who knows what he's doing.'

For a moment Ginny stared at the back of his head. Was he serious?

She realised, with something of a shock, that he probably was. He'd made his first million before he was dry behind the ears. How likely was it that he'd ever had to struggle with the eccentricities of the carry home flat-pack fitted-kitchen?

Okay, so his kitchen hadn't come from the local DIY store on his roof rack. It had been assembled by venerable craftsmen at vast expense. But beneath the slate work surface and the state of the art joinery, the principle was the same.

Probably.

So, the question was, should she tell him that the plinth could be removed to get at the space beneath the cupboard where a runaway hamster might hide?

She didn't think so. At least not yet.

It wouldn't be kind.

While it was perfectly acceptable to suggest a man was a bit pathetic because he couldn't cook—hell, most men were proud of the fact—it was quite another thing to show him up in traditionally masculine skills. It would be like fixing a car while he was busy calling the nearest garage.

It would make him feel inadequate.

Tempting though that was, she decided it would be wiser to leave it to the porter to tell him the good news.

Trying not to grin too widely, she got to her feet, leaving him to contemplate trouble, found some cups and poured out the coffee he'd made.

'Milk?' she offered.

He shook his head. An unruly cowlick of hair slid across his forehead.

'Sugar?'

The same response. The hair slid a little further and her fingers itched to push it back. She tightened them into a fist, forcing them to behave themselves. What was it about this man that made her want to touch him?

Magnetism.

Like gravity, it was an irresistible force and she shouldn't feel bad about it. He had same effect on all females, judging from the number of lovely women he'd dated.

She just didn't care to be that predictable.

Too late. He'd kissed her and the butterflies had not so much fluttered as stampeded around her stomach, while her knees had buckled pitifully. The only difference between her and all the other women being that she'd hated it.

In theory.

The kissing had been…spectacular.

What she had hated was feeling so vulnerable. Being out of control in that way. A pawn to his knight…

'Maybe the porter could help,' she said, reminding herself that a clever pawn could win the game and dragging her mind back to the plan. 'Shall I go and ask him to come up?'

She could do with a little breathing space and once two big strong men started on something like this they'd forget all about her. All they'd want from the little woman would be an endless supply of tea or coffee. Which would leave her free to do what she'd come here for. And now she had his keys in her pocket it wouldn't take her any time at all.

A nervous *frisson* whispered through her body. It couldn't possibly be that easy.

'I'll speak to him,' he said, getting to his feet, taking the coffee from her.

Or maybe it could. That's the ticket, she encouraged mentally. This was men's stuff, after all. Off you go—

'In the meantime, maybe we should try to tempt him out with food?'

What?

'What do you think?'

She thought that was the worst idea in the history of the world, but while she was still trying to frame an answer that wouldn't send those expressive eyebrows of his right up to the ceiling, he said, 'Do you want to go and get some?'

Her smug superior mood evaporated as quickly as it had come. Where on earth was the nearest pet shop? And would it still be open…?

Then reality broke through. He wasn't asking her to pop out to the shops. He was asking her to go next door and get some from her own supply.

Unfortunately, whilst Hector seemed to be achieving almost legendary status in his own right, it hadn't got to the point where she'd started buying jumbo packs of hamster food. Although, if this went on much longer, who could say what she'd do?

'You think something to eat might tempt him out of there?' she asked stupidly. Well, she was stupid. Only the most stupid person in the entire world would be having this conversation. But she needed a moment. She'd thought she had her wits well under control, but while she'd been remembering the way he'd kissed her, how she'd felt, they seemed to have wandered off somewhere and needed to be rounded up quickly.

'Few of us can resist temptation,' he replied.

And he should know, Ginny thought, looking at him as he leaned back against the cupboard, cup in hand, those heavy lids disguising his thoughts.

'What do they eat? Hamsters.'

When she didn't immediately answer he glanced up, regarding her over the rim of his cup.

Damn! She wished he wouldn't look at her like that. As if he knew every single thing inside her head. And then some.

'Anything that comes in a box with "hamster food" on the label,' she offered. It was the best she could do in the time available. 'I have to confess I've never read the list of ingredients.' Which was purely the truth. She'd never read the list of ingredients on any kind of pet food. Unfortunately, she didn't have a box with hamster food on the label. Then, inspired, 'Actually, I think he'd be more likely to respond to a treat.'

'Don't we all. I can't wait to discover what Hector's idea of food heaven might be,' he said. 'Chocolate?'

She pulled a face. That didn't take as much effort as thinking. Impaled on his unwavering blue gaze she was finding it a struggle to breathe, let alone think, remember...

'I've never given him chocolate. It would be terribly bad for him. A grape might do it,' she said, clutching at the straws of memory when the silence had gone on for way too long. Then, when he didn't leap to offer one, 'Or even a raisin.'

'In your own time.'

'I'm sorry?'

'Hamster food, grapes, raisins. I'm prepared to try anything if it means I don't have to start ripping my kitchen apart.'

He'd really do that?

Tempting as the idea was, she couldn't let him do it.

No. *Really.*

'Don't do anything too hasty,' she said.

'Always good advice. Why use a sledgehammer when you can use a nut?'

'A nut would be good,' she agreed. She was positive a hamster would enjoy a nut.

'So now all we have to do is bait the cupboard with something he can't resist and he'll fall right into the palm of your hand.'

He continued to hold her with nothing but the power of his eyes and something about the stillness of the man sent a tiny shiver of apprehension riffling up her spine. It was as if he was saying more, talking about something else.

She needed to move, break eye contact before she broke down and confessed...

'Right.' She turned quickly and stretched up to open one of the high level storage cupboards. There seemed to be a complete lack of the basic essentials. She glanced back at him. 'Where do you keep your dried fruit?'

He regarded her with a somewhat crooked smile. 'I thought we'd already established that I wouldn't know what to do with a raisin, Ginny.'

'What about a grape?' she snapped, losing it just a little as the tension got to her. 'Surely you keep in a plentiful supply of those to feed to visiting goddesses—' along with the champagne '—of the non-domestic variety.'

It was one thing to tell yourself that it would be easy to look this man in the face and tell him lies. It was quite another to do it. She had the feeling that he was toying with her, that she wasn't being nearly as clever as she thought she was. That he knew exactly what she was up to.

Nonsense of course. How could he?

It was just an over-active conscience giving her a hard time.

Well, she knew it would catch up with her sooner or later. She'd just hoped it would be later.

'Find me a goddess—any kind of goddess—and I'll feed her grapes,' he promised. 'Me, I prefer something to sink my teeth into.' He opened the fridge door and then turned to face her, a large red apple in his hand. And she had the strongest feeling that she was the one being tempted. 'How does Hector feel about apple?'

'Loves it!' she said brightly and reached out for it.

With his free hand he caught her wrist, prevented her from taking it. 'I don't want you taking any risks, Ginny.' His voice was soft, but the words sounded more like a warning than any deep concern for her personal safety. 'I don't want you getting hurt.'

'Hurt?'

'The knives are very sharp.' He let her go as suddenly as he'd seized her, turning away to take a knife from the block. With his back to her, she grabbed at her wrist, holding it as if burned. 'Now we wait,' he said as, having put a small piece of apple in the cupboard, he closed the doors.

Ginny realised that she was still rubbing at her wrist as if to remove the imprint of his fingers. Feeling foolish, she dropped it. More than foolish. She was an idiot.

She'd been within minutes of achieving her goal and she'd had the ball snatched out of her hand. Just because she was bothered about messing up Rich Mallory's kitchen.

The man was a multi-millionaire, for heaven's sake. He could afford to have his kitchen put back together by the finest craftsmen money could buy.

He could start again from scratch if he wanted to. It was practically his duty, for heaven's sake. Weren't politicians always going on about how spending money kept the economy rolling…?

'How long?' she asked.

'Long enough to have something to eat.' He bit into the apple. 'I'm hungry. How about you?'

'Not hungry enough to contemplate one of your fried egg sandwiches,' she replied sharply.

'I'm not proud. I went out and earned the bacon. You can cook it.'

She was outraged. 'If you think you're just going to put your feet up like some Neanderthal, while I slave over a hot stove—'

He grinned. 'The woolly mammoth steaks are in the fridge.' Then, as he saw her face, 'But maybe you're right about putting my feet up. I've got plenty of work to do.'

Oh, great! Her and her feminist upbringing. If he used the study she wouldn't be able to get in there. Worse, he'd need his keys.

'Work?' she said, desperately trying to think of some way to retreat from her feminist stance.

'You know how it is. A caveman's work is never done. Spears to sharpen, arrow heads to make…'

He was still kidding? His eyes didn't look as if he was kidding. But she laughed anyway. She wasn't much good at the silvery tinkling kind of laugh that Sophie was so good at. It was more your ha ha ha sort of laugh and Mallory lifted his eyebrows.

Who could blame him?

'No,' she said. 'Don't do that. I'm sorry, I really should keep my sex equality rants for those that deserve them,' she said, with a mental note to practice the tinkly laughter in the privacy of her own home. You never knew when these skills would come in handy. 'You've been so—' So what? Kind? Considerate? Thoughtful? 'Sympathetic.' The words almost stuck in her throat she was smiling so hard. 'You go and put your feet up. Be as Neanderthal as you like,' she said, with about as much sincerity as a double-glazing salesman offering to do your windows for free as a 'demonstration'. 'To be honest, I'd love to have the run of your fabulous kitchen. A real treat…'

Unable to stand the I-really-don't-believe-this expression he was wearing for a moment longer, she opened the fridge door. The cool air was welcome on her hot cheeks. Apart from that it wasn't much use.

She cleared her throat. 'There's just one small problem. You've got milk, eggs—' she opened the box '—make that an egg, and some apples. You appear to have forgotten to bring home the bacon, after all.' She looked around the fridge door. 'Ditto the mammoth steaks.'

'They've all gone?'

He joined her at the fridge door, his chest nudging her shoulder as he leaned forward to check the meat drawer. She had the feeling he knew exactly what was in there. Nothing.

'A hunter's work is never done. So much for putting my feet up. Tell me what you need and I'll walk down to that deli on the corner.'

Rich forced a smile as he said this. He'd been enjoying the cut and thrust of the verbal fencing but suddenly he felt as if a huge weight had settled in his chest. He'd set his trap but deep down he'd been hoping, really hoping, that she wouldn't fall into it. That she'd pick up his warnings—plain enough to anyone with mischief in mind— and back off. Take the hint. Realise that she'd been rumbled and let it go.

He knew it was seriously stupid of him to even give her the chance. He should be giving her as much rope as she needed to lead him to whoever was behind this scam.

Ten years in a cut-throat business should have hardened him up, but the truth of the matter was that she had touched something in him. Something he'd thought he'd buried well out of reach of a pair of bewitching eyes.

His heart.

Of course, there was an alternative.

It was possible that she was as innocent as she looked. His subtle hints might have simply passed above her head unnoticed. In which case his keys would be lying on his dressing table. But how likely was that when she'd made such a transparent excuse to return to his bedroom?

He'd seen her nudge her bag behind the chair.

And it had to have been a key she'd been looking for this morning. Why else would she have been searching his bedside drawer? Why else would she have been so disappointed when she had picked up that earring? She could hardly have mistaken it for a hamster.

She'd jumped as if scalded when he'd caught her in his dressing room. She was smart, but she was too nervous to be innocent. Too nervous to be anything but a first time thief. It still wasn't too late...

'Actually—' he said abruptly, before she could gather her thoughts and provide him with a shopping list, get him out of the apartment '—scrub that. You were right first time. You wouldn't invite me to supper and then expect me to cook it.' He was a fool to himself, but he'd give her one more chance to change her mind. 'Besides, Hector is far more likely to emerge if it's quiet in here. I'll send out for something.'

'You don't have to do that,' she said. 'I've got a lasagne in my fridge.'

'You have?'

Now he was confused. She was supposed to want him out of the way. Wasn't she?

'My mother said she might visit.'

'Your mother the classical scholar?'

'I've only got one mother.'

'Of course.' Then, 'What about your father?' The more he knew about her, he reasoned, the easier it would be to find out why she was doing this.

'No, I haven't got one of those,' she said matter-of-factly.

The impassive response was a mask, he realised. Studied carelessness.

'I'm sorry,' he said, really wishing he'd never asked. He was in enough trouble already without adding a severe case of sympathy to the equation.

'It's no big deal. Single parenthood is practically the norm these days.' The merest suggestion of a shrug. 'My mother was always ahead of her time.'

He thought it was always a big deal, but she lifted her brows, daring him to contradict her.

'So?' she enquired. 'Are you going to risk it? The lasagne?'

'Why not?' Of all the risks he'd taken that day, he suspected her cooking would be the least to cause him grief. 'What's life without a little risk to leaven the mix?'

'Uncomplicated?' she offered. 'I'll go and fetch it.'

'What will you do if your mother turns up this evening?'

'It isn't very likely, to be honest. She's

in London for a conference. Women's issues stuff. She'll probably be talking half the night. Putting the world to rights.'

'For women?'

'Someone has to do it. But if she does turn up, I'll cook something else.'

There was the faintest suggestion of unspoken pain in those few simple words, he thought, impatient for the background check. He wanted to know everything about her...

'How practical you are,' he said. 'Do you need a hand? Carrying anything?'

'No, I can manage to carry one dish from my apartment to yours.' Then, 'Better make that two. I'll just be a minute or two while I sort out some salad and make a dressing.' Then, 'Oh.'

'Oh?'

'I haven't got a lemon—for the dressing,' she said. 'I don't suppose...?'

For a moment he'd thought—hoped— that maybe, just maybe, innocent had been right. Instead she'd been toying with him. His sympathy was misplaced.

'That I've got a lemon? If there isn't one in the fridge, then no.' He was sure she already knew the answer to that one.

'I'm afraid not.' She looked up at him,

the faintest tinge of pink colouring her cheeks, her breasts rising just a little faster than normal. And those eyes were as green as new meadow grass... 'It'll have to be the deli after all, then. If you don't mind?'

'I can manage the walk to the corner,' he replied, keeping his anger under wraps. He knew what she was doing. Why should he be angry? 'Just a lemon?'

'Well, maybe some black olives, since you're going. And some crusty bread?'

'I think I can manage that. I won't be long.'

'Don't rush. The lasagne will take half an hour at least.'

Don't rush! He wanted to grab her and shake her and tell her not to be so damn stupid. Instead he said, 'We could eat outside if you'd like?'

'That would be great. I really like your garden. No pruning,' she said. 'And no pests.'

'There are always pests,' he said.

This was it. She quickly returned with the lasagne, put it in the oven and turned on the heat.

Now. Do it now.

*　　*　　*

Rich didn't hurry. He bought her lemon, some plump black olives, a crusty loaf. There were strawberries too and he bought some of those and clotted cream to go with them.

The condemned felon ate a hearty meal…

He'd tried, done all he could to divert her without actually telling her that he knew what she was up to. He could have dragged it out and declared an abhorrence of pasta, could have refused to be moved from his apartment even for the sake of what would undoubtedly be the perfect salad dressing. He could have insisted on sending out for food.

This morning the idea had seemed positively attractive. An amusing diversion while she thought she was luring him into a honey trap, and he used her to get to whoever was behind this raid.

But once he'd kissed her and diversion had morphed into desire, he knew he couldn't do it. Already he was afraid that her green eyes would haunt him for ever.

He could simply have stopped her, of course. Made it impossible for her to get within a country mile of his disks. That was a temptation, too. But there would be someone else. There was always someone else. He wanted this over with. Most of all he wanted the man who'd sent Ginny to do his dirty work behind bars.

Piece of cake. She'd opened the drawer and there it was. Well, not exactly *there*, on top, just waiting to be picked up. There were half a dozen or so disks and she had to be sure she had the right one. But fortunately they were all clearly labelled.

If she'd really been up to no good, she'd have been very grateful to him for labelling his experimental software so clearly. She'd have expected it to be labelled with some totally innocuous title for security reasons.

Hadn't Sophie said he was security mad?

She shrugged, slapped the disk into her computer and left it to copy on to her hard disk while she took her time about collecting the green stuff for her salad from her fridge. Romaine, rocket…Her hand paused over a new pack of lemons. She could tell him she had found one after all, she supposed. Then she grinned. Bad Ginny. Don't push your luck. And she moved on. Watercress…

She piled it all into a basket with the rest of the ingredients for the dressing. Then, the disk safely copied, she emailed the document to Sophie before returning to Mallory's apartment and replacing the disk and his keys.

It had, in the end, been almost too easy, she thought.

Of course she still had the rest of the evening to get through.

By the time he returned the lasagne was bubbling in the oven and she was assembling the ingredients for the dressing.

'Perfect timing,' he said as he handed her the lemon and, while she squeezed it, he opened a bottle of wine, pouring a couple of glasses before going outside to contemplate his expensive view of the river while the little woman did her stuff in the kitchen.

She swallowed a mouthful of dark red wine.

Chauvinist.

She took another one and on a giddy high, fuelled by the adrenalin charge of the mad risks she had been taking all day, she was almost tempted to remove the piece of apple from the cupboard, let him think that Hector had emerged for his treat. It would serve him right.

Common sense suggested she would be

better advised to leave well alone. Just be grateful that he had, in the end, made it so easy for her. On the point of finishing the glass, she stopped herself and instead began whisking the dressing.

All she had to do was get through the next couple of hours and then it would be over. Sophie was saved from the chinless wonder—at least for the time being. Mallory would, finally, be off for his delayed break in Gloucestershire. And her life would be back to normal.

Great.

So why wasn't she feeling happier?

'That smells good.'

Startled, she nearly upset the bowl, fumbling to hold on to it with trembling fingers.

It didn't help that he was watching her.

As if aware of her difficulty, he rescued her, seizing her wrist to steady it before moving the bowl out of danger.

'I didn't mean to startle you.'

He topped up her glass and taking her hand, pressed the wineglass into it, wrapping his long fingers around hers, holding it there until he was certain that she wouldn't drop it.

If he was trying to help he was going the

wrong way about it, she thought as the trembling, if anything, became worse.

'Good for the nerves,' he assured her. 'Yours seem to be in need in fortification.' He didn't let go but continued to hold her, standing over her, not in any threatening way, but protectively, as if he would save her from herself.

Ridiculous. It was just because her hand continued to shake beneath his fingers, she told herself. He had no way of knowing that her nerves were in tatters because she'd been masquerading as an undercover agent all day. Double O three and a quarter.

Except that it wasn't just the risk of being caught with her hand in his desk drawer that was making her heart pound.

No, this came packaged with blue eyes capable of zapping the ability to reason right out of her brain, a mouth that made her forget all her long kept resolutions, a touch that would have melted permafrost...

He lifted the glass to her lips, tilted it, leaving her with no option but to swallow or dribble. She swallowed... Maybe he was right. The warmth of the liquid seemed to give her strength and finally she was able to take control of the glass.

'My n-nerves are f-fine. Thank you.'

He didn't argue with her, but his brows rose just far enough to suggest that he wasn't about to agree with her. She made an effort to pull herself together. The worst was over. Another hour or two and she could relax.

'Supper will be ready in about ten minutes,' she said.

'Then why don't you bring your glass, come outside and take a proper look at the garden? You couldn't have seen much of it when you were chasing Hector.'

The garden. Of course. Perfect. Such a very English topic of conversation.

So safe.

She seized it with relief. 'I'd love to.'

Except that his wasn't anything like the average English garden; there were no borders crammed with overheated colours, no tubs of vivid annuals, warm and familiar and safe. It was sophisticated, cool, masculine, only softened by a cluster of low growing maples set amongst the rocks that surrounded the pool.

She followed him out across the decking that jutted out over the pool and stood beside him watching the ghost carp drifting up to the surface now that the shadows were lengthening.

'It is lovely. Peaceful,' she said.

He glanced at her. Lovely. Peaceful. But not safe, she thought. Far from safe.

She looked around her, anywhere to avoid direct eye contact with him. A mistake. She simply drew attention to the disturbance of the perfectly raked gravel caused by her earlier intrusion. The scattered leaves broken off where she'd squeezed through Lady McBride's formal hedge.

'You must find the leaves from the McBrides' garden a nuisance in the autumn,' she said.

His smile was little more than a twitch of his lips at this attempt to keep the conversation on a garden party level.

Darling, the delphiniums are a picture…

Slugs have been such a problem this year…

Have you tried nemotodes…

'It's a box hedge, Ginny. It doesn't lose its leaves. Except when squeezed through by athletic hamsters. And their owners.'

'I made a bit of a mess…'

'Don't worry. It'll grow back.'

'Before the McBrides get home? I'm supposed to be taking care of the place, not wrecking it.'

'How long will they be gone?' He glanced at her. 'How long are you staying?'

'Oh, just until the end of September. I have to get back to Oxford before term begins.'

Rich returned his attention to the fish. 'Mrs Figgis said you're a student. Forgive me but you seem a little—'

'Mature?' she interrupted. 'I'm post grad. Working on my doctoral thesis. Doing a little lecturing to keep the wolf from the door.'

That explained a lot. Charity shop clothes. The desperate need for cash. Education was expensive and stealing his software had to be a lot more financially rewarding than stacking supermarket shelves.

'What's your subject?'

Before she could answer, the doorbell rang. He was inclined to ignore it; he was far more interested in what Ginny Lautour had to say, but seizing the opportunity to escape, she said, 'I'd better go and check on supper while you answer that.'

Damn!

His mood wasn't improved when he opened the door and Lilianne, without waiting for an invitation, flung herself into his arms.

'Darling! I'm so sorry! I was a total bitch last night. There you were working all night and I was, well…' She pouted. 'Disappointed.'

And then she kissed him.

CHAPTER FIVE

GINNY heard the woman's voice and she knew instantly that it wasn't Mrs Figgis coming back to ensure the apartment wasn't being overrun with rodents. It was low, throaty and oozing with sex appeal and there wasn't a thing on earth that could have stopped her from looking through the kitchen door.

One glance was all that she needed.

She retreated swiftly, opened the oven door again, determined to give the impression of applied concentration—a total lack of interest in whoever was calling.

Not that he would have noticed her even if she'd been standing next to him, tapping her foot impatiently and reminding him that he'd invited *her* to supper.

With his mouth glued to the scarlet lips of the tallest, thinnest, red-haired creature any man had ever dreamed about—a seven-denier black stocking woman if ever she'd seen one—he wasn't noticing anything.

It certainly put the kiss he'd given her into true, painful perspective. Forget all that outraged virtue. One minor, teasing kiss and she'd fallen for the Mallory charm just like every woman he'd ever glanced at.

Hook, line and sinker.

She hadn't been mad because he'd kissed her without so much as a by-your-leave. She'd just been mad that he'd left her wanting more.

Why else would witnessing the way he kissed a woman he truly desired—the serious effort he put into it—cause real physical hurt? Like being stabbed with a blunt knife. A few minutes ago she'd been congratulating herself that she would be out of his apartment in an hour or two.

How easy it was to fool yourself.

Well, she'd been saved by the bell and now she wouldn't even have to stick around another minute.

Lucky her.

She shut the oven door, glanced around the kitchen, her gaze lingering on the cupboard beneath the sink. She should do something about that...

Consign poor Hector to myth where he belonged.

But not right now. Right now she was

out of here while he was too occupied to stop her. And she picked up her bag and headed for the door. Mallory's eyes swivelled in her direction as she passed them.

'Don't mind me. I'll come back when you're not so busy,' she said. Then, 'The lasagne's just about ready.' If he was still hungry after devouring his unexpected visitor... 'Don't let it spoil.'

It was the woman who spoke, breaking off the close quarter engagement to demand, 'Who's she?'

'I'm meals-on-wheels,' she snapped back before he could answer, twitching her shoulder out of Mallory's reach as he made a grab to stop her. Sheesh. She knew he liked variety, but surely one woman at a time was enough, even for him. 'Don't forget to put the dish to soak.'

He called out something as she let the door slam behind her. It might have been, 'Wait!'

That was the trouble with those heavy fire doors, she thought. You couldn't hear a thing through them. Not even the most peremptory of commands from an arrogant male.

Safely on the other side of the door, she muttered, 'No thanks. I'll come back when there isn't a queue.' Then, deciding that hanging around might not be such a bright idea, she took the lift down to Sophie's apartment in search of a little sanctuary and a large glass of something warm and steadying for her nerves.

Little enough in return for all the risks she'd been running in the last twenty-four hours.

Actually, it wouldn't hurt to check that the document had arrived safely. Ensure that Sophie didn't delete it again. Copy it on to a disk for her, even, so that she could take it into work tomorrow.

After that, all she had to do was 'find' Hector hiding out in one of her own cupboards, apologise to Rich Mallory for her stupidity—a note under the door should do it—then she could erase all thoughts of magnetic millionaires with electric blue eyes and seductive kisses from her mind and put the whole unnerving affair behind her.

Rich was beyond angry. He was furious. With Lilianne for turning up on his doorstep uninvited. With himself for allowing her to catch him off guard. Most of all with Ginny for taking the opportunity to waltz out of his apartment when he'd had serious plans for her.

He'd had her right in the palm of his hand. Well, if not the palm, somewhere pretty damn close and with a couple of glasses of wine and some of her own good cooking to relax her, she might have been coaxed, teased, wooed into indiscretion.

What kind of indiscretion scarcely mattered. One way or the other she'd be in his pocket rather than someone else's.

They'd both be using her but—whether she'd appreciate the fact or not—he would do her the least harm.

What kind of harm she might do him was something he didn't care to think about. He hadn't given a woman so much undivided attention since...

Since he'd been twenty years old and blindly in love with a fellow student who was as lovely as she was devious. She'd walked away with a software program he'd written and bought herself a job with it.

It had been a hard lesson. But well learned.

Until Ginny Lautour had looked up at him with a pair of bewitching green eyes.

Damn it, he didn't believe that Hector existed in anything but imagination—had never believed he existed—yet he'd still been prepared to pull apart his kitchen on the off-chance that she was telling the truth.

He'd really wanted her to be telling the truth.

Even when she'd been raiding his study and he knew for a fact she was lying, he'd found himself remembering the way her eyes had looked when he'd kissed her. And, like a small boy who'd been told by an older cousin that Santa Claus didn't exist and in his heart of hearts knew that it was the truth, he still wanted to believe...

But instead of Ginny, all dither and blush, he'd got Lilianne—clearly regretting her fit of pique and seizing the first opportunity that presented itself to put the clock back to midnight—flinging herself into his arms.

He didn't know what flowers Wendy had sent her, or the message that had accompanied them, but his secretary clearly knew her stuff because they had certainly worked.

He could scarcely complain. It wasn't her fault that the timing was off.

If Ginny hadn't seized the opportunity to escape before he'd managed to extricate himself from a truly vice-like hug, he could have eased Lilianne out with a regretful shrug. Okay, so he'd have looked like a complete heel. But a reputation for having a short attention span where women were concerned had its uses. No one expected any better from him.

As it was, she'd taken advantage of his slow reactions and while he was still caught between holding off Lilianne or going after Ginny and hauling her back, his unexpected guest had made herself at home in the kitchen and was now well into the domestic goddess routine.

And if she'd noticed that there were two used glasses she had clearly decided that discretion was the better part of…whatever.

Well, what had worked once, would undoubtedly work again. Only this time he would have the courtesy to warn her. That way he could dispense with the flowers. And any further misunderstanding.

Leaving him free to go after Ginny.

'Lilianne, I'm sorry—'

She'd tied a tea cloth around her clinging dress and had lifted the bubbling lasagne from the oven to the island. She licked the tip of her thumb then looked up at him.

'No more apologies,' she said. 'All forgotten. Gosh, this looks good. It could just do with a bit longer. Just long enough for a glass of that scrummy wine, perhaps?' Then, when he didn't immediately move to pour her a glass, 'How clever of you to have someone bring in home-made food. You must give me her number.'

'You should have telephoned,' he persisted, refusing to be distracted by the flutter of eyelashes. 'I'm busy.' He wasn't lying. He was working very hard to protect his interests and he'd always put work first, as she'd already discovered. But he'd never subscribed to the rule that you couldn't mix business with pleasure. 'That's why I've had to put off my weekend away.'

'I know. Your sister called me.' So, it was a conspiracy. He'd been right to avoid Gloucestershire. 'She told me you were up to your eyes in work.'

'She was right.'

'If you'd warned me last night...' She lifted her beautiful shoulders in the most elegant of shrugs. 'I'm sorry. I shouldn't have overreacted that way but I was mad because I'd planned something really special.' She lowered her lashes, moved closer and began to play with his shirt buttons. 'For us.'

He caught her hands. Stopped her.

She pouted. 'Darling, I promise you, I do understand that business has to come first. I won't run away again. We'll eat, then you can do whatever you have to and afterwards, well, I'll be waiting no matter how long it takes...'

He bit back the word that flew to the tip of his tongue. They'd been playing this game for a couple of weeks and it wasn't her fault that he'd suddenly lost interest. Confronted with an armful of beautiful and willing woman, he didn't understand it himself.

'I'm sorry, Lilianne, but I'm afraid that isn't an option.'

She smiled—it was the sultry, straight to hell smile that had snagged his attention in the first place. Practised, artful and so obvious compared with the startled innocence of Ginny's wide-eyed shock as he'd freed half of the McBrides' hedge from her hair.

As he'd kissed her.

Or maybe Ginny was a better actress.

Was it possible to blush on cue?

Lilianne, perhaps sensing that she didn't have his full attention, raised her hands to his shoulders and looked up at him from beneath lashes that owed as much to cosmetics as nature. 'Rich, please…'

'I'll call you a taxi,' he said. And disengaged himself.

Sophie wasn't sitting at home chewing her highly polished nails to the quick and worrying about her best friend—or her job—Ginny discovered. She wasn't home at all.

She was probably having a high old time in some club, or in an expensive restaurant having her hand held by some drooling male.

Nothing new there.

The only surprising thing about Sophie was that she hadn't been married to some rich minor aristocrat by the time she was nineteen. She had the kind of fragile beauty that was meant to be cosseted by a man who adored her. She was born to live surrounded by lush acres of parkland, with beautiful horses, decorative dogs and at least four adorable children. She would, of course, have a capable staff to deal with all the messy stuff.

Sophie herself had had it all planned out, with a shortlist of suitable candidates. It had been her sixth form project, receiving a lot more attention than her A-levels.

Then, while Ginny had taken her four starred As and gone off to university, Sophie, with no intention of spending any more time cramming her head with useless knowledge, had taken a 'gap year' to work through her list and decide which of her prospective mates was going to be the lucky man. But somewhere along the way she'd taken her eye off the ball and been sidetracked by the serious business of having fun.

Sophie and Rich Mallory were made for each other, Ginny thought sourly. If she'd been truly cynical she might have thought that Sophie had got herself the job at Mallory's company in order to attract his attention.

Apparently not.

Maybe Sophie's father had a point. Ginny frowned as she took the stairs up to the McBrides' apartment. What had happened? Why…?

She got no further than the 'Why…?' before she spotted the man himself standing at her door. If she hadn't already mentally got him tucked up with the luscious female with the scarlet lipstick—and she'd been making a real effort not to think too much about that—she might have been paying more attention and been able to duck out of sight.

Too late. He'd heard the door, turned and spotted her while she was still trying to decide what to do. Short of dashing back down the stairs—and how would that help when she'd have to come back sooner or later?—she would appear to have no option but to smile and try to look pleased to see him.

She hoped she was more successful than he was. His expression suggested that he was torn between wishing he were somewhere else—preferably on a different continent—and, well, it was hard to say. He had more control of his facial expressions than she had. But maybe he was just a bit pleased to see her.

Or maybe that was wishful thinking.

Why on earth would he be pleased to see her? She was causing him nothing but trouble, for heaven's sake?

And why would her heartbeat lift a little—actually quite a lot—at the thought? What a ridiculous idea. He was the kiss-and-run type of man she most despised.

She'd got that charge from the mental challenge, but that was over, she reminded herself, even if he didn't know it yet. And her heart was pounding a little harder than usual because she'd run up the stairs. That was all.

Even so, the temptation to tell him, right now, that her little wanderer had returned and he could forget all about it was intense. But somehow she didn't think he'd be convinced. Not after the way she'd cut and run...

He would want to see for himself.

She had the feeling that he'd insist.

No. She'd let him off the hook tomorrow when he had other things to occupy him and he'd just be glad it was all over. Meanwhile, on with the performance...

'Have you found him?' she asked, making a real effort to look hopeful.

'Found him?'

'Hector. Why else would you be ringing my bell?'

'I'm ringing your bell because we were going to have supper.' He reached out, seized her elbow and, without bothering to check if she was still interested, he steered her firmly in the direction of his apartment. 'Your tactful withdrawal was beautifully done but quite unnecessary.'

'Oh, but it was necessary,' she said. 'There isn't enough for three.' Even if one of them looked as if she could survive for a week on a lettuce leaf.

'Lilianne isn't staying for supper. And, for future reference, I prefer to make my own arrangements in that department.'

'Oh.'

Bother.

Even as she thought it she was having to force down the corners of her mouth so that she wasn't grinning like a Cheshire cat.

'I'm so sorry. I didn't want her to think...' Well, no. Realistically, she wouldn't. 'What did she think?'

'That you were a caterer who produced home cooked meals for single males incapable of doing it for themselves.'

The lines that bracketed his mouth deepened, the corners of his eyes creased in a sunset fan. He was clearly not the least bit worried about keeping his amusement to himself at this mistake.

'You know, there could be a major business opportunity there,' he continued. 'In fact, Lilianne wanted your telephone number. If you're interested, I'll pass it on.'

'Lilianne knows enough single men to make it worth while, does she?'

'Cat,' he said, but if anything his amusement increased.

Oh, drat. Jealousy was such a give-away. The last thing she wanted to do was give him the impression that she was keen to become yet another scalp on the crowded bedpost of his life.

'Yes, well, in that case I'll, um, dish up, shall I?'

'Good plan.'

He checked the cupboard while she removed the lasagne from the oven. Again. It was beginning to look decidedly crispy at the edges

'No sign of Hector,' he said.

She glanced at the open cupboard. 'It might be a good idea not to keep opening the door,' she advised. 'You wouldn't want to frighten him off, would you?'

She shouldn't do it, she knew, but Mallory just seemed to bring out the worst in her. A 'worst' she'd never encountered before. Since she couldn't admire the man for his heroic properties, the attraction just had to be pure lust. Although maybe 'pure' wasn't an entirely appropriate adjective. Since it was a first for her, she couldn't be certain.

Whatever, it offered a very good reason to keep her mouth shut and a safe distance between them. It also explained why she was finding it so difficult to do that.

'You think we should just leave it?' he asked. 'Wait and see if the apple goes?'

She was burning up with lust. He was just concerned about a hamster infestation. It figured.

'If it goes we'll know he's there,' she pointed out, confident in the knowledge that he wasn't. 'Then we can decide what to do.'

'You mean we can dismantle my kitchen?'

'That's it,' she said, quite prepared to do a little teasing of her own. But she was too quick with her smile.

'Perhaps we might try a humane trap before we do anything too drastic,' he suggested.

'You are no fun, Richard Mallory,' she said, as she divided the pasta between two dishes, sucking on the end of her thumb where hot sauce had bubbled on to it.

When he didn't immediately come back with some smart answer she looked up, prepared to laugh, but he wasn't smiling. Not one little bit. He'd shut the cupboard door and was just looking at her, his face unreadable.

For a long moment he was so still that her breath caught in her throat and couldn't find a way out.

Nothing moved. It was as if the world was on hold, waiting, so quiet that she could actually hear the blood pumping through her veins.

Then, when she thought that something explosive had to happen—would have welcomed something explosive, anything had to be safer than that dangerous silence—he reached out and took her wrist.

'Did you burn yourself?'

She couldn't say. His touch sizzled far more dangerously than hot pasta sauce, fizzing through her veins like a fuse, and she was beyond framing a coherent thought, let alone a straight answer. He didn't ask again, but simply looked for himself before lifting her thumb to his lips very briefly. Then he turned on the cold water and held it there so that it ran over both their hands.

Relief—or maybe it was the effect of cold water—released her from the breath-holding tension and she managed a choked, 'Thank you.'

He checked her hand then looked up, still not smiling. 'No problem,' he said.

On balance, she thought that he was less dangerous when he was smiling. Than not. She made a move to pull away, retrieve her hand, but he didn't let her go.

'No problem with your hand, anyway. However, if you think that taking a kitchen apart is fun, Ginny, you need some serious lessons in how to enjoy yourself.'

Only then did he release her, turn and pick up the plates. 'Can you bring the wine and the glasses?' he asked.

It wasn't an offer then.

What should surely have been relief felt rather more like regret; she was sure that if you needed coaching in fun he would be the man to get you through your finals with a starred first. The only kind of result she'd ever been willing to accept.

'I think I can handle that,' she replied, holding the glasses against her breast to stop them from rattling.

Rich carried the plates, kicking off his shoes as he stepped up into the little Japanese pavilion which had been built under the protection of the apartment wall, glad of a little cool air to clear his head.

Why was it that when Lilianne had sucked on her thumb he'd seen only the obvious sexual invitation? Something designed solely to tempt and as such—beyond instant gratification of the most basic kind—of very limited appeal? Or, in this instance, a complete turn off.

Whereas when Ginny had used the same gesture he'd known instinctively that it was an innocent reaction to a burned thumb rather than a seductive gesture contrived to turn him on.

And contrarily, the effect on him had been inflammatory.

He put the plates on the low table, then retraced his steps and rescued the glasses and bottle, which looked as if they were about to slip from her grasp. Shaking a little himself as their hands collided, fingers became entangled.

'Thanks,' she said, a smile wobbling briefly on her lips. 'I'll go and fetch the salad.'

'No, you sit down.' She looked ready to bolt and he wasn't giving her another chance to escape. 'I'll get it.'

'Oh, right. Don't forget the bread. And the dressing. I should have put it in a jug. It'll need another whisk...'

He said nothing, just waited. She kicked off her shoes without embarrassment or making some stupid comment, then knelt gracefully on one of the cushions by the low table.

Her full figure would look wonderful in a kimono, he thought. Her hair in a knot, wisps escaping about her face. He imagined how it would be to pull loose the pins, have it tumble over his hands...

'Is that it?' he said.

'That's it,' she said. Then half-opened her mouth as if she wanted to say something else. But thought better of it and closed it again.

'I can do it,' he said. 'I may have caveman tendencies, but I'm not completely stupid.'

At least he hoped not. He'd given her the rope, but where had she run with it the second she'd escaped? Not back to her apartment, obviously. But not very far. There hadn't been time.

'Actually, I was going to say we need forks, too.'

He returned with the dressing properly whisked and in a jug and everything else they needed, then he too folded himself up on the cushions before pouring her a fresh glass of wine.

'We should be eating sushi,' she said. 'I should be whisking tea.'

'This will be fine. I just hope all your hard work hasn't been spoiled by the delay.'

'Just leave the crunchy bits round the edges.'

'Right.'

He offered her salad, took some himself. Taking his time. Complimenting her on the food—well it *was* good—and keeping it impersonal. Not pushing for conversation.

Dusk was settling over the city, the sky was the soft violet of a late summer evening. 'I love this time of day.'

'It's better in the country. The air is fresher and you actually get to see the stars.'

'You live in the country? Whereabouts?'

'I live in Oxford. But I drive out to the country when I can. I can't wait to get back.'

'Then why are you flat-sitting in London?'

'I needed to use the British Library for some research. This is the only way I can afford to stay here. I'm really very lucky to have such a wonderful place rent-free.'

It was chance, then? That she was next

door. Had she been targeted because of where she was staying? Or had it been planned that way from the beginning? She knew Philly McBride slightly. How had she met her?

'What's your subject?' he asked.

'The Hero: Myth or Reality?' There was not sufficient light to tell whether she was blushing. But he was almost certain she was.

'And have you come to any conclusions?'

'I'm still working on it.'

'What else do you do?'

'Sorry?'

'You study, lecture, drive into the country, keep a pet hamster. I'm trying to round out the picture here. See the whole woman. Where do you live? Have you got anyone important in your life? Do you like the movies?'

'That sounds more like an inquisition. What about you?'

'My life is an open book. My business world is regularly featured in the financial pages, my personal life a constant fascination for the diary columnists. But I'll concede the point. You answer a question, you get to ask one. Is that fair?'

She shrugged. 'Okay. I live in rooms in college.'

'Do you enjoy that?' She raised her eyebrows. 'You get to ask me a supplementary.'

'Yes, I like it. And it's convenient.' Then, 'How do you feel about having your life under the microscope? Being the object of endless speculation.' She sounded as if she really wanted to know. As if...

Lautour. The name finally clicked.

Her mother was Judith Lautour, the militant feminist who had chosen some brilliant scholar as the father for her baby. An early experiment in genetic engineering. Could two geniuses raise an infant prodigy...?

The outrage in the press that had sent the woman's books into the best-seller charts for weeks.

'The truth?' he said, when the silence had gone on too long. 'It used to incense me, but really, what's the point? It's mostly fiction, after all, a daily soap opera, a little excitement over the morning coffee. You know how it is—a single man with a fortune has to be married for the amusement of the masses, preferably more than once. Or outed as gay.'

'You seem to have done pretty well in avoiding both those fates.'

'The first is a question of time. Or rather a lack of it. Women require a certain amount of attention. To feel needed. If they're neglected they tend to wander off and look for someone more attentive.'

'You're telling me that you're not the one who loses interest?'

'Work it out for yourself, Ginny. If I was sufficiently interested, I'd make more effort to ensure they didn't feel neglected. Last night I got involved in work and forgot Lilianne existed.'

'She appears to have forgiven you.'

'She left me a very rude note. She deserved an apology but that's it. End of story.'

'Oh.'

'As for the second... Well, when you've been photographed with enough lovely women, no one bothers to ask the question.'

She lifted her eyebrows. 'Is that *all* you do? Have your photograph taken?'

'You've had your supplementary, Ginny. It's my turn.'

'Have I got anyone important in my life?' she prompted.

'No one who cares enough to put a ring on your finger,' he answered for her, unable to resist the opportunity to provoke something more than a yes or no answer.

'Marriage is such an outdated institution, don't you think?'

'You follow your mother in more than scholarship, then?'

She hesitated. 'Not entirely,' she said. 'I wouldn't make her choices.'

'To be a single parent?'

'Out of passion, maybe. But she used a sperm donor, you see? She is gay, you see.'

Forget one question—there were a dozen forming on his lips. Who? Why? What kind of childhood had that been? How she'd lived with the curiosity, the inevitable intrusion. He kept them to himself.

'Actually, I don't,' he said, finally.

'Don't see?'

He saw, felt for her, wanted to reach out and wrap her in his arms and hold her, protect her...

He shook his head. 'I don't take the view that marriage is an outdated institution. No matter what the relationship. I believe that a lifetime commitment should be honoured with due ceremony and the total understanding of the contractual obligations of both parties.' He'd been unexpectedly moved at the solemnity of the undertaking between his sister and her husband as he'd witnessed their signatures in the register. Ginny looked doubtful and he shrugged. 'Like any business undertaking,' he added. He did, after all, have a reputation to live down to. 'The wedding ceremony, no matter how simple or extravagant, provides all that.'

'With a jolly good party afterwards, with the pick of the bridesmaids for dessert.'

And he found himself wishing he hadn't made that comment about business. Marriage, if it was done well—and there was no point in doing it any other way—was a lot more important than any business undertaking.

'Maybe I'm old-fashioned, but I believe in order.' Then, 'No, my question is—'

'You've had your question!'

'On the contrary. You suggested one, I discounted it and then you sneaked in another one. It's definitely my turn.' And he found a grin from somewhere. 'Twice.'

He was a lot better at this kind of stuff than she was, Ginny realised. She'd laid down the rules of this engagement, but too late she realised that he wasn't the kind of man to play by anyone's rules other than his own.

He'd always bend them to his convenience, taking complete advantage of her lack of any experience in this kind of double-edged banter to draw out the kind of information that she normally kept under lock and key.

She never told strangers about her mother. She left the tittle-tattle to other people and they'd never let her down yet.

But she was learning.

This time she didn't leap in, even though he paused, like the gentleman he wasn't— gentlemen didn't kiss girls they'd only just met—offering her the opportunity to contradict him. Instead she kept a wary silence, clamping her jaw shut and refusing to break it even when it stretched to snapping point.

Refusing to give him the satisfaction.

Refusing to... 'What?' she demanded, unable to bear it a moment longer. 'What do you want to know?'

His eyes creased in a smile—dammit, she knew he'd smile—and he said, 'I want to know what you're doing tomorrow.'

CHAPTER SIX

HER caution had been well placed.

Ginny, for just a few tantalising moments, had been remembering how it felt to be back in control. Well, almost. Her heart rate had still been a little rapid, but the tremor that had been as unpredictable as the aftershock of an earthquake since Rich had kissed her thumb had begun to subside to manageable proportions. Now she was right back where she'd started.

Doing? Tomorrow?

Using extreme care—so that it wouldn't clatter against the china—she placed her fork on the side of her plate. A sip of wine would have helped the sudden dryness in her mouth, but she didn't dare pick up her glass, certain it would shatter between her fingers.

Like Richard Mallory she believed in order, had determinedly avoided the turmoil and mayhem with which her brilliant but unconventional mother had so carelessly blighted her childhood, her adolescence.

She never wanted to be out of control, ever again.

She'd tripped once, fooled by the easy treachery of a warm smile and kind words, betrayed by a yearning to be wanted, needed, not as some experiment but just for herself.

She had the emotionally bloodied knees to show for it when the object of her affections had sold his story to a tabloid newspaper.

Now she would only ever step out of line, take risks, for Sophie; despite her friend's shallow 'playgirl' exterior she'd always been there with an outstretched hand whenever the world had seemed a black and lonely place. If the tables were turned, Sophie would do this for her. Without question.

So she determinedly ignored the excited hammering of a heart that should have, did know better and hunted out one of the stock answers that she kept about her for just such occasions.

It took rather longer than it should. But it had been a long time since she had actually needed to use one of them.

If she didn't come up with one soon, he'd know it was just an excuse...

Except she didn't need an excuse. The truth would do perfectly well. 'I'm working tomorrow,' she said. Then, because, she also had an unconquerable curiosity—the kind that had always taken her to the top of the class, won her academic scholarships—she couldn't quite stop herself from adding, 'Why?'

Rich had been expecting an excuse. Had been interested to know what she'd come up with on the spur of the moment. The length of time she'd taken to answer suggested that, put on the spot, she hadn't found it easy. Then, before he could congratulate himself on his cleverness, she'd turned the tables, waylaying him with a question to which he had no answer. Or, at least, not an answer he was prepared to confront. Or admit, even to himself.

'Oh, nothing.'

Nothing? If it was nothing why ask? He could see that was what she was thinking, and he was wondering the same thing himself.

There he was all lined up to ask her thoughtful, probing little questions, encouraging her to reveal her innermost thoughts, secrets, desires and without warning he'd been asking her what she was doing tomorrow. Not as part of some well-thought-out strategy, but as if he was going to ask her out on a date, for heaven's sake.

As if he was desperate to spend more time with her.

Bed, sex…well, yes. No problem. He didn't need any emotional commitment for that. But this felt…emotional…

Not that it mattered. He was safe enough. He'd known she would come back with some feint and he was right. She'd got what she wanted. She had no reason to spend any more time with him.

So why ask 'why'?

To gain a little thinking time he struck a match, and lit the candles inside a simple glass candleholder so that the garden retreated into the darkness and only her face reflected back the soft light.

There was, he would be the first to admit, nothing about her to make him look twice under normal circumstances. She didn't make the slightest effort with her appearance. She'd clung to spectacles when most girls would have abandoned them for contact lenses. She wore no make-up. There were no artificially applied sunshine streaks to draw attention to her mousy hair. No clothes cleverly cut to display her body to advantage.

There was not a thing about her to shout to the world, 'Look at me, I'm beautiful…'

If she was trying to look invisible—and of course she was—she couldn't have done a better job.

Maybe that was what made him keep looking. The contradiction between the fact that there was, apparently, nothing hidden, nothing false about her coupled with the powerful conviction that her lack of artifice was, in itself, a disguise. Whatever it was, it worked for him.

With nothing more than the soft luminescence of her skin in the twilight and green eyes full of secrets, she had his full attention.

She also, he was almost certain, had a disk containing his newest software project. Or at least, she thought she did, which amounted to the same thing.

She had a disk. One she'd stolen from him. And the minute she used it he'd have her. At which point she could speak to the police, or tell him everything he wanted to know.

In the meantime, he told himself, spending time with her would be no hardship. And whether it was the head of Mallory plc or Rich Mallory the man who was driving that thought he wasn't going to argue with it.

'If I have to dismantle my kitchen,' he said, finally answering both her questions—the one she'd asked and the unspoken one he'd read in her eyes—'I'm going to need an assistant.' He paused just long enough for her to think about that. 'Someone to hand me a screwdriver when I need one,' he added provokingly, because he loved the way she never failed to rise to a little provocation. 'But of course if you're too busy...'

Of course she'd be too busy. Hector was pure invention. How apt, he thought, that someone familiar with the Homeric myths should adapt the 'Trojan Horse' scenario to get inside his security 'fortress'.

How clever.

And the slightest shiver rippled down his spine, a *frisson* of excitement.

Was that the attraction? The knowledge that this was a lot more than the usual kiss-chase, played out on a purely physical level. It was a game of wits.

Right now she thought she'd won, that

she'd got what she was looking for. Why would she waste any more time on him?

There wasn't a reason in the world. Tonight her little runaway would be 'found' and in the morning he'd find a polite little note under the door informing him of that fact, apologising for all the trouble she'd caused him. She'd probably even make a point of thanking him again for being such a good neighbour. And do her level best to avoid him for the rest of her stay. It shouldn't be that difficult. Their paths would never have crossed if she hadn't discovered, somewhat belatedly, that the bedroom she was searching was occupied...

And with a jolt he realised what that meant. Someone he trusted must have told her that he would be away.

Ginny was finding it harder and harder to remember that she was in Rich Mallory's home under false pretences. Talking, sharing a meal, a bottle of wine—and she'd better not have any more of that!—she'd begun to relax. He was so easy to be with. To laugh with.

Now she was being given the chance to spend the morning cosied up with the darling of the diary columns, babe magnet of the month—any month—all-round hunk and multi-millionaire. Okay, so the cosying would be in the kitchen. Screwdrivers and spanners rather than smoked salmon and champagne. But it was Rich Mallory's kitchen and anyone would tell her that she'd be a fool to say no.

Except Sophie, of course.

But while some hitherto unknown, untapped feminine need was urging her to let the work go hang—she could work any time but this was a once in a lifetime opportunity that should not be missed—the responsible, prudent part of her brain, the part that had never let her down, counselled instant retreat.

She found herself stalling.

Okay, so he was flirting with her. Big deal. Clearly the man couldn't help himself. Or was it that he felt it was expected of him, that she'd be disappointed if he didn't make an effort? On neither account should she feel particularly flattered.

Even if she was foolish enough to succumb to Mr Ever Ready's charm on the kitchen floor it obviously wouldn't mean a thing to him. While she...

She'd be an even bigger fool to fall for it.

Prudent was right. She did not need this.

'Richard,' she said, and feeling the power of his name on her tongue her concentration wavered and common sense went walkabout. But then he did one of those is-this-actually-going-anywhere-soon? things with his eyebrows and she dragged her wandering wits back into line. 'You do not have to rip apart your kitchen,' she said. 'Really. I'll go out first thing tomorrow and buy one of those humane traps. It'll be kinder all round.'

The minute the words had left her mouth she knew she'd made a mistake. He shifted slightly—it wasn't anything as positive as a shrug—and she had the uneasy feeling that he'd been waiting for her to say something of the sort.

'You're very relaxed about this,' he said, confirming her suspicions. 'In your place most women would be frantic by now.'

Clearly he believed men were made of sterner stuff. Remembering how her roommate at college had panicked, running around like an idiot in a similar situation… No forget similar—nothing in the history of the world had ever come close to this.

'I don't see how getting frantic will help,' she replied. That was supposed to sound calm, the wise words of a woman in total control of her world. It just sounded defensive.

'It won't,' he agreed, 'but it's a natural reaction. Nothing to be ashamed of. Aren't you afraid the poor little thing will starve?'

Now she knew he was going out of his way to provoke her. Make her feel unnatural and cold-hearted. She knew she was neither of those things. That if Hector were real he would have grapes and the fattest nuts and whatever else his little heart desired. And that, curiously, made his accusation easier to deal with.

'Not imminently,' she replied. 'He's the best fed hamster in London. Probably.' He couldn't refute it. 'Glossy of coat, bright of eye—'

'And with a turn of speed that wouldn't disgrace an Olympic hurdler.'

'You've got it.'

'Doesn't that kind of energy require constant feeding?'

She was getting seriously irritated with him. 'The hungrier he is, the more likely it is that he'll take your bait,' she said, through teeth that weren't totally gritted, but it was a close run thing.

'He hasn't shown any interest in that apple.' And she had the feeling that she was the one being baited.

'Well,' she said doubtfully. 'It is a red apple. He prefers the hard, green ones.' Oh, good grief...

'Is that right?'

His eyes glittered in the candlelight, as if ransacking every word, every inflection for...something. And again she had the feeling she was treading on ice so thin that a warm breath would melt it.

'How old is he?'

'Two,' she said, saying the first number that came into her head. 'And a bit.'

'Isn't that quite old for a hamster?'

'It's not young,' she agreed with rather more hope than conviction since she had no idea how long a hamster might be expected to live. She should have done some serious homework before embarking on this foolishness, she realised. It had just never occurred to her that she'd be drawn into an in-depth discussion on the subject. In fact, the whole thing had got way out of control. Then, with a jolt, as she saw where he might be going with this, 'You think he's dead, don't you?'

She didn't have to look horrified. She was. She kept her teeth clamped tight shut to avoid the groan escaping. How on earth could she have said something that stupid?

Before she knew it they'd be into the second verse of All Things Bright and Beautiful and raising a little plaque in Hector's memory...

She had to get away from him before this nonsense went any further. She'd put a note under his door first thing. Panic over. Hector found. It was perfectly possible that he'd doubled back while she was fighting her way through the hedge... Found home and food and then curled up and taken a very long nap after his exertions...

'This has been great,' she said. 'Good food, good wine, good company, but I really have to go.' She didn't wait for him to go through the motions of encouraging her to stay, but quickly got to her feet. Then she said, 'Ouch!'

She was a sofa person. The bigger and squashier the sofa, the better. Sitting on the floor oriental-style had given her a dead-leg and, as it failed to support her, she went back down as fast as she'd risen. But with considerably less grace and upsetting a glass as she tried to save herself.

He was beside her before she could blink. 'Are you hurt?'

'Not unless you count my dignity,' she said, biting back a groan and forcing a smile. 'Just give me a minute for the circulation to get going and I'll try that again.'

She rubbed her leg in an attempt to speed up the process, but Rich stopped her. 'Keep still and lie back.'

What?

'I'll be fine,' she said quickly, determined to do nothing of the sort. She would hop if necessary. Even as she sent the message to her legs to stop behaving like a pair of wet hens and do as they were told he ran his hands gently over her foot.

'You'll be fine quicker if you'll lie back and leave it to me to get the circulation going.'

Of course she would. It was foolish and stupid to make such a pathetic fuss. He was being kind, that was all. Just because he'd kissed her once didn't mean a thing.

If he'd enjoyed the experience he'd have done it again.

And it wasn't as if she could even feel anything very much, she protested when 'prudent' and 'common sense' waved the caution flag from their corner. Her leg was numb. But she shivered, nonetheless, as he propped her foot against his chest and began to work on her ankle, his fingers searching out the pressure points.

'I tend to forget that sitting like that for any length of time is an acquired skill,' he said matter-of-factly and glancing up at her.

So matter-of-factly that she realised just how foolish she was being. He wasn't going to leap on her the minute she was out flat. He had Miss Scarlet Lipstick for that kind of thing. Ready, willing and...

She blocked out the thought. And started breathing again.

'Okay?' he asked after a moment or two.

'Umm,' was about all she could manage as he slowly kneaded the life back into her ankle, her calf.

More than okay, actually.

In fact, her only coherent thought at that moment was one of gratitude for a seriously painful evening of mutual leg waxing that Sophie had inflicted upon her earlier in the week. At the time—between screams of pain—she'd protested that she didn't need smooth legs, that no one ever saw her legs.

Sophie—taking advantage of the fact that she was living upstairs to put her through one of her 'it's-time-you-made-more-of-an-effort-with-your-appearance' evenings—had just grinned and carried on, saying that it was one of the things you did, '…like wearing sexy underwear. Just in case.'

Her response, that it was *clean* underwear you were supposed to wear 'just in case' only brought an enigmatic smile from Sophie. But the next day a courier had arrived at her apartment bearing an elegant box containing a set of underwear that defined the word 'sexy'. The handwritten note had simply said:

This beats 'clean' any day, wouldn't you say?

And right now she was really, really wishing that instead of her plain, sensible underwear she'd put on one of those black lacy thongs and the matching bra, a miracle of engineering that would do spectacular stuff to her cleavage…

Stupid. As if he'd notice…

But anything more rational was impossible just at that moment because there was a war going on inside her head.

The bit of her brain where all the sensible stuff happened was tut-tutting furiously and telling her to forget about sexy underwear. What she should be wearing, it warned, was that good solid pair of jeans.

A skirt, it continued with finger-wagging persistence—even a long skirt—was no protection against the infiltration of masculine fingers intent on the sensuous kneading of her flesh.

He'd reached her knee now and the bit of her brain that seemed to frizzle whenever Rich came close, the bit that sent warm flushes to her cheeks, buckled her knees and made her breasts leap and send out 'touch me' signals, went into overdrive. It was saying lie back and enjoy this, Ginny.

Umm. Enjoying it was definitely the more attractive option.

He glanced up. 'Am I hurting you?' he asked.

She blinked. Had she actually 'ummed' out loud? Maybe she was letting herself get a little bit *too* relaxed. 'Er, no.' Then, in case she had, and because she didn't want him to think she'd 'ummed' with pleasure, she qualified it. 'Not much, anyway. You're doing a good job.'

A glint in those blue eyes, a tiny tuck in the corner of his mouth, suggested he knew exactly what he was doing.

'Is the feeling coming back? Are you getting pins and needles?'

She was getting something, but it wasn't the torture of pins and needles. More like a tingling warmth that was seeping through her veins, licking over her skin as he held her calf in his palm, stroking her leg from knee to ankle, hand over hand in long smooth strokes.

A tingling warmth that was pooling and settling low in her belly.

'It's not unbearable,' she managed.

Far from unbearable. His touch was gently probing, tender, setting light to nerve-endings in a seductive caressing of her skin…

Then he shifted his attention to her thigh and somewhere deep within her a panic button was pressed. This was too intimate… Too dangerous…

Too late; the warm pool at the centre of her being heated up, spreading slowly through her until her entire body was liquefying with pleasure at his touch. She didn't care how far he went. It wasn't just her breasts that were begging to be touched…

A moan of longing slipped past the

guard of her lips. Rich looked up, his face all shadows, unreadable.

In the silence, a question.

One to which her body's answer was a resounding 'yes'. But to which 'prudent', slipping through unnoticed in the confused turmoil of her brain, was already slamming the doors, putting up the shutters, refusing to listen.

'Oo…ch,' she said. A sound somewhere between a moan and an ouch.

It was unbearably loud in the quiet of the small circle of candlelight and when he looked up again his eyes were no longer glittering. They were more grey than blue now—soft and smoky… It was probably the effect of the candles. Except they were burning still and clean…

'The feeling is back?'

'Absolutely,' she said. And because she had to do something, say something to shatter the tension, 'How did you learn a skill like that?'

'Like what?' He sounded vaguely confused too. 'Oh, sitting on the floor. I spent some time in Japan,' he said, and stopped what he was doing. She immediately wished she'd kept quiet. 'How's the other leg?' he asked.

Oh, terrific. Now he could read her mind. That would never do. It was definitely time to make a move.

'Fine,' she said quickly. This time he apparently believed her and she was instantly sorry. Confused—it was what she'd wanted, wasn't it?—but sorry.

She'd had both legs waxed and it seemed a shame to waste all that pain...

'I'm sorry, Ginny.'

'No, it's fine,' she said quickly, feeling guilty about that 'oo-ch'. Pretending that he'd hurt her. 'I love your pavilion, the whole thing—'

'I didn't mean to upset you. About Hector,' he added, because she hadn't got the faintest idea what he was talking about. And clearly it showed.

Who? Oh, *Hector*.

Oh, drat. He wasn't apologising for the unconventional seating arrangements. And he hadn't been fooled by her 'oo-ch'. She had to face it, he'd probably done this dozens of times. Hundreds of times. He'd clearly known exactly what he was doing and it certainly didn't deserve an ouch. Or even an 'oo-ch'.

It rated nothing less than an X-certificate moan.

'No. No, really, I'm fine,' she said with forced brightness, pushing her skirt modestly back into place with hands that were visibly shaking, sitting up, backing off a little. 'He'll be back tomorrow, you just wait and see. Hungry, sorry for himself and worn out.'

She could almost see the little bedraggled creature. Another minute and she was going to be in tears. She sniffed. She was already close...

'Thanks for the first aid,' she said.

'I should be thanking you,' he said, rising to his feet, offering a hand to help her up. But not denying the nuisance bit, she noticed.

That, somehow, made it easier to place her hand in his but, as he pulled her up in one smooth movement, in a *déjà vu* moment she was once again confronting his shirt buttons; it was the dressing room all over again.

The scent of well-laundered clothes, good soap, warm skin. The closeness of man she desired. Shockingly.

It was an anything-could-happen moment when he might have swept her into his arms and kissed her senseless. And she, shockingly, knew that she just might let him.

It wouldn't take a lot.

She wasn't far from senseless already.

Just far enough to take a step back before the scene went into re-run, before Rich took off her spectacles again and, without so much as a by-your-leave ma'am, he was kissing her again. She forced herself to let go of his hand.

It shouldn't be this difficult...

'How is it?' he said.

Dazed, confused, she said, 'What?' Then, 'Oh, the leg. Fine. Good as new.'

His hand was still there, an offer of support should she need it, as she slipped into her shoes. But she wasn't about to play the helpless female just for the pleasure of his touch. Instead, she made a move to go.

'Do you have to go?' His hand, resting on an upright beam, cut off her escape. 'Can't I tempt you to a little brandy?'

'Yes... No...'

He smiled, making her confusion worse. 'I think I understand that. But you see my problem?'

He had a problem? 'What problem?'

'What am I going to do with that bowl of strawberries?'

About to suggest he tried them on Hector, she restrained herself. She was in enough trouble already.

'That's not a problem, Rich. If you can't eat them I'll be happy to give them a good home.'

'That wasn't the right answer,' he said, his voice a little ragged, his eyes suggesting that he had plans along the lines of one bowl of strawberries, one bowl of cream and some slow indulgent dipping.

She was clearly going mad.

'I'm sorry. It's the only one you're going to get. I've got a pile of work to do.'

He let his hand drop but didn't immediately move to let her pass.

'Someone reminded me today that work never goes away. That you shouldn't let it rule your life.'

'That is true and when I've got time I'll give it some thought. But right now I've got a very tight schedule and a limited amount of time.' The truth at last. 'Thanks for being such a great neighbour,' she said and, rather to her surprise, meaning it. 'I've been a total nuisance.'

Actually, when he wasn't morphing into serial lover mode, he *was* a great neighbour. She quite liked him. Really. In fact, she couldn't see what Sophie's problem was with him. If she needed a husband he had all the necessary qualities…

Money.

Good looks.

A short attention span.

No, Sophie knew what she was about.

And so did she. Clearly that showed in her face, too, because this time when she made a move towards the open French windows he stood aside, but she hadn't taken a step before his hand was at her back as he fell into step beside her.

It felt possessive, as if now that he'd touched her, kissed her, she was in some way his. Which was plainly ridiculous. Why would he even want her, when he had a fabulous redhead at his beck and call?

It wasn't personal, she reminded herself. It was just something he did.

Or maybe it was simply her overheated imagination beginning to hallucinate. She could hardly blame it after the day she'd put it through. She collected her bag from the kitchen, momentarily escaping his touch as he took her at her word and got out the strawberries and the carton of cream, before walking her across the hall to her own door, placing them into her hands.

She felt awkward taking them. As if she should invite him in to share them. Make coffee.

But he was probably counting on that. How many times had he used that routine before? Get real, Ginny. Why would he have to bother? Anyone but you would be at his feet by now.

Anyone but her. Right. She was a one-off. An original. A failed experiment.

'Thank you,' she said. 'These will go down well with a couple of chapters from Homer.'

'No, Ginny, thank you for the great food. Should you decide to go into business, I'll place a regular order.'

'Maybe I will. It probably pays a lot better than ancient history.'

'People always need to eat.'

It was that kind of clear vision that had made him a millionaire. Probably. 'I'll bring your dishes back tomorrow,' he said.

Maybe it was the thought of him turning up unannounced on her doorstep, but her hands, a moment ago quite steady, were suddenly incapable of juggling the bowl and the cream and inserting the key into the lock. Not without inviting catastrophe.

Seeing her problem, he took the key from her and unlocked the door before dropping it back into her palm, just the way he had with the earring that morning.

Had it only been that morning?

It seemed light years ago.

'Don't worry about Hector, okay? We'll find him.' And then he held her shoulders lightly and kissed her. On the cheek. A brush of lips, nothing more, and before she could say anything smart, or stupid, he was on the far side of the hall at his own door. He turned, looked back. 'Don't work too late, Ginny. Try and get some sleep.'

Since he was waiting for her to go inside, shut her door, she did just that, leaning back against it and letting out a long, slow breath.

'Get some sleep,' she muttered to herself, rubbing the flat of her palm over her cheek to smooth the down that seemed to be standing on end. Her fingers lingering on the place where his lips had brushed her skin. 'Oh, that'll be easy...'

Forget orange juice and scrambled eggs. That man just tapped straight into the National Grid every morning and powered up. That could be the only possible explanation why he only had to touch her for every cell in her body to light up and fizzle like an over-loaded power line.

Rich leaned back against the door. Groaned. What on earth was the matter with him? His body was throbbing. Hard and aching. But not just for sex. If he'd just wanted sex he'd have been in bed with Lilianne right now. She couldn't have made it plainer that the 'chase' was over. She'd been hot for it.

It was something of a shock to his libido to be told to lie down, forget it, he wasn't interested. But it was suddenly and blindingly obvious to him that he hadn't been doing anything more than going through the motions for a long time. What had Wendy said about an endless parade of women out of the same mould?

She'd exaggerated. It hadn't been endless. But there had been too many women and not nearly enough relationship.

Ginny Lautour wasn't out of any mould. She was an original.

He'd known it the minute he'd opened his eyes and seen her, one moment covered with blushing confusion, the next as cool and collected as a duchess at a garden party. Known it when he'd looked into her eyes and she'd lost it again...

How many women could invent a hamster—would have the imagination to invent a hamster—and then make him seem so real that he wanted to believe...? Almost did believe...

How many women could attract him with nothing but a ridiculous propensity to blush and the power of her eyes?

Only one.

It was time to stop fooling himself.

He wanted sex, but he wanted a lot more than that. And he wanted it with Ginny Lautour.

He'd had enough of the who-can-pretend-best verbal fencing. With his hands on her ankle, her leg, on the sweetest dimpled knee that it had been a crime to hide beneath jeans or a long skirt; it was her he wanted. And he wanted her now.

He wanted to undress her, taking his time about it, exposing the reality of her body in the slow, sensuous dance of love. He wanted her naked, her pale skin gleaming in candlelight. He wanted to see her blush as he kissed her, touched her. He wanted to see her eyes blazing like emeralds as, with his hands, his mouth, his tongue, he stripped away all her deepest secrets and lay bare the reality of her soul.

He shook his head.

There had been a moment, the stillness between one heartbeat and the next, when he'd thought it would be possible. But something, the smallest movement, a retreat from intimacy, if not the longing for it, had warned him that it would be a mistake.

And when he'd looked into her eyes, no longer a bright pellucid green but a swirling cloudy grey, he'd seen something more.

Her body might have been willing, her head might be urging her to do it—it was the most reliable weapon in the arsenal of the female spy—but her heart would not have been along for the ride. And that told him more about Ginny Lautour that any dossier from a security consultant.

Someone had hurt her. Made her afraid to let go, no matter how loudly her body was clamouring for her to go for it. He didn't care that she'd stolen from him, what the cost in thwarted desire or financial loss, he wanted every part of her. Total meltdown.

He wanted her sure and certain of her

power. Demanding, assertive, taking what she needed, living up to the hidden fire he'd glimpsed in her eyes.

Deep inside him, deeper than he'd ever gone, he knew that if he could take away the fear and give her the courage to let go, to leap off the edge rather than fall or be pushed, then he wouldn't have to ask for anything in return. She'd give him everything he'd ever wanted.

And he was way beyond the name of a software pirate.

At that moment he wanted Ginny Lautour with a bone deep need, with a hunger that had stirred not just his body but his soul. It was a feeling so new, so unexpected, so disturbing, that he knew he should be thankful that she hadn't fallen for his tricky little ruse to get inside her apartment. Grateful that she'd sent him packing, given him a chance to get his head straight and his body under control.

Grateful, hell.

She was already so deep inside him that he doubted he would ever be rid of her. He wouldn't be human if he didn't want her in his bed. Now. This minute.

What he was going to get was a long cold shower and another night alone with his computer. And Wendy was right; it was no substitute.

CHAPTER SEVEN

GINNY had told Richard Mallory that she was going to work and she'd meant it. She wasn't the kind of girl who swooned when a man looked at her as if he wanted to undress her slowly, and then do unimaginable things to her...

She pressed the cold glass bowl to her cheeks.

Not her. No way. Not that she'd had much experience of men doing anything of the kind. And what she did have served only to warn her against being foolish enough to fall for it ever again.

Not that he'd sell the story to the tabloids. At least they had that in common. Too much publicity, too little truth.

Even so, it took a minute to insert a little metaphorical steel into backbone before she managed to lever herself away from the door, dump the strawberries and cream in the fridge well out of the way of temptation, and head for the safe harbour of her desk.

Work was the answer. It always had been.

Once she immersed herself in Homer she would forget all about his long fingers caressing her legs. No problem. She could do it. Piece of cake.

She booted up the laptop. Called up the file she'd been working on. It would anchor her mind, stop it from wandering off on little side trips of its own, daydreaming about the totally delicious way Richard's dark hair curled around his ears, for instance. Or that little crease that appeared at the corner of his mouth just before he smiled...

And she refused to indulge herself in those little tingle-in-the-pit-of-the-stomach moments that happened whenever she looked at him. Whenever he looked at her. Whenever she thought about him...

'Stop that!'

Talking to herself wasn't good either...

She took a deep breath and began to read the notes she'd made the day before so that she could put them into some kind of order. Order was good.

Okay. She began to read.

Her eyes moved across the words. Individually they were good words. Probably. Collectively they weren't actually making it past the disturbing sensory stimulus that still lingered, despite all her best efforts to banish them from her thoughts.

Nipples tingling as they brushed against her shirt. The disturbing ache low in her abdomen. Her mouth full and soft...

When she'd read the same paragraph three times and still had no idea of what it said, when her notes disappeared and the screen-saver began to dance across the screen, the words 'piece of cake' seemed to beat out a mocking rhythm to her heartbeat.

Furious with herself, she went into her bathroom and splashed cold water on her face. Then her neck. At which point she understood why people took cold showers...

She was not going to take a cold shower. What she was going to do was make a cup of tea. Herb tea. Raspberry and echinacea, which according to the label helped with alertness.

Staring at the pretty pink tea, she was confronted with the fact that she was already alert. Very, very alert. Positively zinging with alertness in places that were doing absolutely nothing to help her concentration on mythic Greek heroes. The only man she was concentrating on was not a myth, nor was he Greek. And he certainly wasn't a hero.

Okay. Change of strategy. She'd call Sophie, who could—when she put her mind to it—distract for Britain. Her ditzy friend could also confirm that the document had arrived safely, that her job was saved. Then she could put Richard Mallory, computer disks and hamsters right out of her mind.

There was no answer. Of course there wasn't. It was Friday night and Sophie would be out partying as always. For once in her life Ginny wished she'd gone with her.

She left her a message, asking her to check her email and call her in the morning.

Then she poured away the herb tea, which did not taste anywhere near as good as it looked and smelled, and decided what she really needed was not a cold shower, but a warm bath—this time with a few drops of lavender oil to counteract the stresses of the day. That would deal—once and for all—with any lingering alertness.

The warm, sweet-scented cocoon of water did its job. Lying back in the big tub she felt totally relaxed, almost weightless. The gentle pressure of water against her breasts, her abdomen, thighs, eased away the tension until her entire body felt soft and blissfully yielding. Then she closed her eyes and let her mind drift. And it wandered right back to Richard Mallory and the way his hands had stroked the life back into her leg. Only this time he didn't stop at her leg...

She leapt out of the bath, mindless of the water pouring off her body and on to the floor. Enough.

She did not desire Richard Mallory.

Any more than he desired her.

Beyond the fact that she was female and therefore a target for masculine vanity. The extra I-am-irresistible gene that men seemed to get packaged with the Y chromosome. Along with an innate urge to prove it to the world.

That he could have, almost certainly would have, sweet-talked her into his bed she did not doubt. He was, physically, a man with enormous personal appeal. He was also a man of infinite experience and her almost instant response to him—almost!—left her in no doubt that if he'd turned up the sexual volume he could have drowned out all her rational arguments. Her own traitorous body, with its built-in programming to reproduce—programming that even her mother had been unable to resist—would have been his biggest ally.

But it would have meant nothing to him. Less than nothing.

If, a week later, he remembered her at all it would be because she was a bit odd. The flaky girl with the hamster. Not much to look at but, what the heck, he hadn't been doing anything else that evening...

Bastard.

She pulled on a pair of washed soft baggy cotton pyjamas, shook loose her hair, brushing it until her scalp tingled, stimulating the blood supply, getting the oxygen circulating around her brain.

Then she gathered up all her clothes and dumped them in the wash basket, methodically going through the pockets.

In the purple shirt she found a shrivelled up piece of hedge. And the earring. Her hand closed over it and she smiled. Wrong. He could have been doing something else.

She put the earring in a safe place and then she went back to work. The Hero: Myth or Reality.

And suddenly she wasn't so sure.

Rich had two things clamouring for his urgent attention.

The report from the security people who were running a check on Ginny stacked up on the in-tray of his fax machine.

And the need to check the mail waiting icon on his computer.

Of the two, the mail waiting was the most important. And the one he least wanted to look at. If the disk she'd taken had been accessed without an authorisation code it would prompt a scan on the computer running the program and then, using the latest wireless technology it would, like ET, 'phone home' and download the results into his laptop.

It would deliver a list of the documents on the rogue computer. All the names in its address book. He would know who she'd emailed and when. More importantly, he would also know to whom she had copied his disk.

She'd had the time, while he was shopping for her lemon, to send it to half the world.

And suddenly he didn't need a cold shower.

Ginny Lautour was not some innocent young woman, he reminded himself. She was the enemy. No, not 'the' enemy. *His* enemy. She was intent on stealing from him, laughing at him with those dangerous green eyes while she was doing it. Bewitching him with those dangerous green eyes.

His mind hadn't been his own since he'd switched on the light this morning and caught hcr—likc a rabbit momentarily frozen in the headlights of a car—guilt written all over her face.

The speed with which she'd recovered herself should have been enough to warn him that she was no innocent. That the blushing confusion was all an act.

The only thing about her that hadn't been fake was that moment when she'd backed away from intimacy. Or was he fooling himself again? She already had everything she wanted; she didn't need to do the whole Mata Hari bit.

Except that if she'd been that good an actress she wouldn't need to steal software to finance her studies. She wouldn't need to do that anyway. Judith Lautour might be a single mother but she was hardly poverty-stricken. She was never off the television or out of the best-seller charts.

He made a pot of strong coffee and carried a mug, black and sweet, through to his study where he checked his laptop for the telltale email.

Nothing.

He sat down. Double-checked. There was no problem with his connection. Mail had been dropping into his inbox all evening—some of it from his Chief Software Engineer, marked urgent. But there was no download from his doctored software, nothing to suggest unauthorised access to his secrets.

He ignored the mail from Marcus—it was Friday evening, for heaven's sake, and there was nothing so urgent that it couldn't wait until Monday morning—took a mouthful of coffee and considered the options.

Maybe she hadn't used the internet to pass it on. She'd been out somewhere. Not far, though. There hadn't been time. Could she have met someone outside? Or used the regular mail? There was a post box on the corner...

He picked up the internal phone and called the porter. 'Mike, have you seen Ginny Lautour go out this evening? The girl who's flat-sitting for the McBrides?'

'I haven't seen her since I came on duty at six. Is there a problem upstairs?'

'No, nothing for you to worry about.' He picked up the sheaf of papers from the fax machine and began to flick through them. 'It's just that she was looking for something earlier. I thought she was at home but she isn't answering.'

'If it's urgent I'd normally suggest trying Sophie Harrington's apartment. They're good friends—'

'Really?'

She had a friend who lived in the building?

'Well, yes, they are a bit of an unlikely pair, but they were at school together according to Miss Harrington.'

'What number is her apartment?'

'Seventy—'

Next door to Cal and Philly McBride? Ginny had said she knew Philly slightly.

'But Miss Harrington hasn't come in yet.

Do you want me to ring through to Miss Lautour?'

'No. Don't disturb her. She's probably working. It'll do tomorrow.'

Harrington? He replaced the receiver, trying to recall why the name was familiar. He was sure he'd seen it recently. Then he shrugged. It would be listed in the entrance lobby. He'd have seen it dozens of times…

Then he stopped thinking at all as he saw the newspaper article that had been attached to the report. She wasn't hiding behind spectacles but looking up into the camera and laughing. Relaxed, happy, in love and full of the joy of life. Eighteen, nineteen…

The headline read An Experiment That Failed…

There was a brief rehash of the circumstances of her birth, the endless speculation at the time about who her father might be, every crazy thing her mother had ever done. But then it got down to explaining how Judith Lautour's much vaunted experiment in genetic manipulation had been a total failure. That, far from being a superwoman, her daughter was just another undergraduate going through the university mill. According to her current boyfriend, the one who'd obviously supplied the photographs, she was more interested in going to parties, getting drunk and making up for lost time now she was allowed to mix with the opposite sex than working for her degree...

That it wasn't true, any of it, was clear from the very thorough job the security agency had done.

She'd only had one boyfriend as an undergraduate. One had probably been enough. Rich was pleased to note that he hadn't made it to the second year, despite his early promise. Someone had cared enough to make sure he'd paid for his betrayal and his lies.

But then the newspaper wasn't interested in the truth, only in giving Judith Lautour a sandbagging; it didn't matter who got hurt in the process.

And he had thought he knew what it was to be done over by a diary columnist with nothing to fill his page.

He continued to read. No father. Well, he already knew that. A mother who gave her all to her causes and who'd switched her daughter from day school pupil to boarder at her expensive public school when she herself had taken to camping out with her fellow protesters.

She hadn't been well served by those who should have loved her, he thought, and he called the agency, widened the area of enquiry, stressing the urgency, before giving up on the coffee and pouring himself a glass of Scotch.

He crossed to the open French windows and looked out over the lights of the city, attempting to make sense of what he'd learned. There was, apparently, no man in her life. She was quiet, studious, hard-working. No one had a bad word to say about her.

So what the devil was she doing searching his apartment?

He wandered outside and breathed in the scent of…lavender.

Ginny tried a few breathing exercises to focus her mind and block out the distracting presence of Richard Mallory a few yards away from her on the other side of the wall.

Work. That had always been the answer. It would answer now…

She stared at the screen, typed a few words, deleted them, started again. After ten minutes she stopped. Okay. It was going to take more than breathing exercises.

She picked up the latest Lyndsey Davis novel. A treat she'd been saving as a reward for work well done. If she could lose herself in that...

She couldn't.

Realising that she was in deep trouble, she flicked on the television and found that instead of the film she saw only a pair of blue eyes, creased in laughter. Blue eyes, still and watchful. Blue eyes heating up as he'd taken off her spectacles and then, slowly and deliberately, kissed her.

She leapt to her feet, prowling the apartment. This was ridiculous. How dare this man invade her head and, ignoring the 'no trespassing' sign, evade all efforts to evict him, set up camp and make himself at home?

No. That wasn't right.

This wasn't his fault. Nothing that had happened today was his fault. She couldn't even blame Sophie. If she'd said no, absolutely not, no way, that would have been that. But Sophie was her friend and knew she could count on her when she was in trouble.

Except this time it wasn't only Sophie who was in trouble.

She'd been asking for it from the moment she'd stepped over Rich Mallory's threshold. From the moment she'd been caught and hadn't immediately owned up, confessed, told the truth instead of coming out with that nonsense about a missing hamster.

She was in the wrong and she deserved everything she'd got...

And boy, had she got it.

She ran her fingers across the keyboard of her laptop. But it was hopeless to even think of work and she pulled off her spectacles and tossed them on to her desk, pinching the bridge of her nose between finger and thumb.

Sleep would be an equally hopeless endeavour and unfortunately it was way too late to put on a pair of jogging pants, go out into the streets and run the man out of her thoughts. Instead, she flung back the French windows to let in fresh air and stood looking out at the lights of the city spread before her, but the sounds coming off the river—music, people having fun—just made her even more restless.

Warm milk? Would that dull the senses?

She opened the fridge door but, confronted by the bowl of strawberries, ripe, red, luscious, her senses revolted. They didn't want to be dulled down, they wanted excitement...

She tore open the carton and, taking a strawberry, she dipped it into the thick yellow cream. Then bit into it.

Not exciting enough, but good. Very good.

She nestled the cream carton in the centre of the strawberries and wandered barefoot out into the garden. She didn't have a Japanese pavilion like her disquieting neighbour, nowhere to sit cross-legged and meditate, quietly recover her equilibrium.

Tough. Her equilibrium had been having everything its own way for far too long.

She padded across to an elegant white painted love-seat, sat down, put up her feet and stretched out her legs.

If she was going to be disturbed, she decided, might as well be *thoroughly* disturbed and enjoy the experience.

She picked up a huge strawberry by the hull, dipped it into the carton of cream, then, tilting her head back, she lowered it to her mouth, biting it off at the stem. Cream and juice dribbled out of the corner of her mouth and she laughed, catching it with the tip of her tongue.

From beyond the hedge she heard a faint sound.

More than a sigh, less than a groan.

Richard Mallory. All the danger, excitement a girl could ever want...

Heart hammering, she lifted her head, sucking her fingers clean, using the time to gather self-possession about her like a blanket before she turned to look at him.

It was a waste of time.

Nothing could prepare her for the sight of his dark figure backlit by the soft light spilling out of the open windows. His face was all shadows that were only deepened, intensified by the pale glimmer of cheekbone, the hard edge of his jaw, the halo effect around his dark curls.

Then he lifted his hand and the light caught the heavy cut-glass tumbler as he lifted it to his lips.

In her head she tasted the Scotch on his lips and her body dissolved at the thought.

'Want to share?'

Had he said that or had she? Or were the words locked in her head where only she could hear them?

There was a long moment when he

didn't move. When she couldn't decide whether she was supposed to answer him or whether she was waiting for him to answer her.

Then he moved slowly towards her, pushing his way through the box hedge. Somewhere in her throat a protest formed—she was supposed to be taking care of the McBrides' apartment, not wrecking it—and then died. The hedge would grow back. It was what hedges did...

Rich said nothing, just placed his glass into her hand before lifting her feet to make room for himself on the bench. Once beside her he dropped her legs across his lap. He had the thighs of an athlete, firm and strong, the denim slightly rough beneath her ankles. His hands were cool against her instep as he absently stroked her feet, regarding her with a level penetrating gaze that offered no clues to his thoughts.

If they echoed her own she was going to get all the excitement she could handle.

His eyes never leaving hers, he reached out and helped himself to a strawberry from the bowl on her lap, dipped it in the cream, once, twice, before carrying it to his lips. For a moment he held it there and she watched the cream move slowly over the green frill of the hull and spill on to his thumb. Then he bit into it. Ginny, who'd been holding her breath, let out a little squeak, then buried her face in the glass and took a mouthful of Scotch.

It was a mistake.

For a moment she thought she'd choke as air and spirit hit the back of her throat simultaneously, but somehow her epiglottis managed to sort out what went where. The air filled her lungs and the Scotch found and warmed her stomach before spreading out through the rest of her body like wildfire.

'That's a fine single malt,' Rich said after watching her silent efforts not to splutter and cough. 'You're supposed to sip it, savour it. Slowly.'

Her throat was still trying to disentangle her vocal cords and she didn't even attempt to reply.

It was okay. He hadn't finished.

'I should be cross with you.'

'I'll sip in future,' she said quickly. Then, apparently driven by some centuries deep feminine need to disturb this man in the same way he profoundly disturbed her, she slowly drew her fingers across her left breast in a large cross. 'I promise.'

There was something deeply satisfying about the fact that he too seemed to be having some difficulty with the simple mechanics of breathing. She wanted him breathless. She wanted him lost for words, unable to reason, at her feet, an open book that she alone could read.

She was, quite clearly, losing her mind.

He eventually managed a slightly hoarse, 'I'm delighted to hear it.' His face, though, betrayed nothing of his thoughts. 'But I wasn't referring to the whisky. I was referring to the fact that you lied to me.'

Oh…*Hector!*

He'd found out what she was up to. Forget excitement. Forget Rich Mallory at her feet. What she was about to get was trouble. With a capital T. In fact, she was up to her neck in the deepest dunghill—

'You told me you had to rush off to catch up on important work—'

What?

'And yet here you are, sitting in the moonlight, indulging yourself in nothing more taxing than eating strawberries.'

He was talking about supper? About the

fact that she'd rushed of, scared out of her wits by her own burgeoning desires?

'I meant to work,' she said quickly. Any belief that she was off the hook was mitigated by his stillness, by the soft, slightly ragged quality of his voice. She suspected that, if anything, she was in deeper trouble.

This was simply picking up the scene where they'd left off. As if there had been no interruption. The air was as loaded with expectation, the connection between them as intense as that moment when he had looked up, his eyes asking a question to which she had had no answer. Except run.

She hadn't run far enough.

'I tried to work,' she said. 'Honestly.' Then, 'I was seduced away from Ancient Greece by a sinfully delicious bowl of strawberries and cream.'

'Now that I know what it takes I'll put in a regular order. But you still misunderstand me. I have no problem with the indulgence.' He picked up another strawberry by the frilly green hull, dipped it into the cream. 'My only objection is that you are alone.'

And he it offered it up to her lips.

It was an age-old gesture and Ginny recognised it for what it was, understood that to accept the fruit from his hand bore a deeper, more primal significance. Every inherited female instinct warned her that, in taking the food the hunter had brought her, she was accepting the hunter. It was ancient and primitive and had no place in the equal opportunities twenty-first century.

But in the soft light of a gibbous moon it cried out to everything that was female within her, kindling elemental needs, yearnings; bypassing all the barriers she had so carefully erected against hurt. It stirred her damped down sensuality and sent it licking hotly along her limbs, seeping through her body and into her soul, blotting out all memory of hurt or pain.

Filled with a desire she scarcely understood but recognised as something unexpected, something powerful, a force that if she were bold enough she could take and use for herself, rather than something fearful to be held in check, she leaned into him and, taking hold of his wrist, her eyes never leaving his, she bit into the strawberry.

The explosion of taste, texture, pure pleasure filled her mouth. The animal warmth of his skin, the pure male scent of him overriding the sweetness of the fruit, the ragged sound of his breathing, reached out and grabbed her remaining senses and shook them into shocking Technicolor awareness.

And this time the soft, low sound that wasn't quite a moan, but was definitely more than a sigh, came from her.

She was suddenly hungry, starving, ravenous for life and, guided purely by instinct, she bent her head and licked up the trickle of juice and cream that was running down his thumb.

He dropped the half-eaten fruit and, his hand open, he reached out and cradled her cheek in the palm of his hand, his thumb brushing against her temple. For a moment neither of them moved, spoke.

Below them in the darkness the city rumbled and roared and went, unheeding, about its business. Ten storeys above the river the only sound was that of her heart beating, the only light came from the heat in Rich Mallory's eyes.

His fingers slid through her hair, tangled in it, wrapping it over his fist until he had her his willing prisoner. Then he lowered his mouth to hers. She expected a fierce and hungry passion. Anticipated it. Craved it.

He touched the corner of her lips in a

butterfly light kiss. Gentle, sweet, yet her intense awareness of him magnified his touch a thousand times. Every inch of her skin flushed with pleasure, felt as if it were reaching out to be caressed, wantonly inviting the most intimate of kisses.

It was shocking, thrilling, a sensory experience beyond anything she had experienced, could ever have dreamed of.

Then he licked along her lower lip, his tongue dipping into her mouth to taste her, taste the sweet fruit she'd eaten, and in return she confronted the reality of that bone-melting moment of her imagination as she tasted the whisky on his tongue.

CHAPTER EIGHT

RICH was losing it.

He was losing it in the scent of warm skin, silky hair that owed nothing to artifice, a womanly body naked beneath the thin cotton of her pyjamas.

His mouth moved over the yielding sweetness of Ginny's lips, and the detached part of his mind—the part that never quite switched off from whatever project he was working on—couldn't compete with the overload of sensations and it shut down.

Losing it...

Who was he kidding? He'd lost it—lost himself—the moment he'd set eyes on her stretched out on the garden seat, a ripe strawberry poised above her lips. It had been a private moment of pure indulgence and her unconscious sensuality had left him breathless.

He didn't care who she was, what she wanted from him. He knew only that he desired her, craved her, wanted her in some way that was so different, so unfamiliar, that he was floundering like a boy who'd just discovered that girls were not an entirely bad thing, but hadn't worked out quite what to do about it.

And similarly afraid.

Ginny Lautour was different and this was a step into the unknown. A step from which, once taken, there would be no turning back.

She did not come wrapped up as a glittery parcel, scented, made-up, dressed by some expensive couturier—a gift to be opened and enjoyed at leisure in a mutual pact where both parties knew exactly what they were getting. He doubted she'd ever been than cynical.

It shocked him just how cynical he'd become…

She was not just another woman, a passing attraction that temporarily snagged the small—very small—part of whatever attention he could spare from work. A little arm candy to keep his company profile high in the media.

Her clothes were awful, her hair was a mess, she wore no make-up and yet she made every other woman he'd ever met seem dull, monochrome, totally forgettable.

Confused, he drew back. What exactly was it about this woman that set his senses alight? Not her hair, surely? He opened his hand, let its silky length slide through his fingers and she nuzzled her head against his palm like a contented cat. He almost thought he could hear her purring.

Not even her clear, translucent skin innocent of anything more seductive than a smear of strawberry-stained cream on her cheek, although that was surely different enough...

He rubbed his thumb over the pink smudge, let it wander over her neck, her throat.

And it couldn't be her body. Her clothes were chosen to conceal rather than tempt. Even now she was wearing what looked like a pair of kid's cotton pyjamas...

Thin cotton pyjamas.

His hand, with a mind of its own, brushed lightly over her breast, his palm grazing a hard, jutting nipple.

That was all she was wearing. There was nothing between them but a few buttons and a cast iron certainty that he had not intended to go beyond a teasing kiss.

He wanted her to trust him. He wanted

her to know that he would never do anything to hurt her.

His fingers, with a life of their own,
slipped the first button.

'Ginny…?'

Her name was a question. This was going faster and further than he had ever intended and he needed to see her eyes, to
know what she was feeling, what she
wanted. He wanted all of her, not just her
body, but something more that would be
just for him…

'Look at me.'

Somewhere, a long way away, a telephone began to ring and, with the tiniest of
sighs, she obeyed him and opened her eyes.
In the moonlight they were liquid, seduc-
tively dark. He'd thought his body could
not be more aware, more responsive. He
had been wrong…

'You were right,' she said.

'Right?'

'Strawberries definitely improve with
sharing.'

…more wrong than he could ever have
imagined.

'Or maybe it's the Scotch and the kisses
that make them taste so good,' she said.
She handed him the glass, which dealt with

the wandering fingers, then lay back against the arm of the seat, smiling dreamily. 'Do you hear bells?'

He set the glass down at his feet. He didn't need whisky. He was getting all the stimulus he needed just looking at her.

'Bells?' Yes, he'd heard bells. The whole of the earth was ringing with the sound... 'I'd like to take the credit, Ginny, but I think you'll find that the ringing in your ears is the telephone.'

She looked momentarily startled, then grinned. 'I knew that.'

'Sure you did,' he said, and felt like grinning himself. Ear to ear like a big kid. 'Do you want to go and see who it is?'

'I'd rather sit here, sharing strawberries and looking at the moon.'

It was a good plan, except that if they stayed there the strawberries were not going to be playing much part in the proceedings... As for the moon, all he had to do was look into her eyes.

Deep, dark with hidden depths, he'd been going down for the third time with no possibility of ever coming up again when he'd been saved by the bell. Not that she seemed in any great hurry to see who was calling.

He understood that.

He didn't want to go anywhere, either. It took an enormous effort of will to remind himself that this was not something to be rushed, lift her legs from his lap and get to his feet, trusting in the dark to hide just how stimulated he was.

'The moon isn't going anywhere.'

Cool air rushed into the empty spaces where Richard's body, his hand, his mouth, had moments earlier been stoking up her personal central heating system, warming her from the inside out. And Ginny shivered.

'Clearly you have a very poor grasp of astronomy,' she said. 'The moon, let me tell you—' about to confound him with astrophysics, she discovered that she was fairly shaky on what, exactly, the moon did '—isn't about to stay put for our convenience.'

'Neither is whoever's calling you.'

No. She willed the telephone to stop, but it continued to ring and ring and he offered her his hand to help her up.

'It's probably your mother hoping for some of your excellent lasagne,' he reminded her. 'And a bed for the night.'

Damn. She'd forgotten she'd told him

that. How like her mother it would be to turn up on the one occasion she wasn't wanted. Especially when the alternative had been so much more enticing. But, wherever the evening had been going, the journey had been interrupted for the second time.

Once by her out of fear. Fear of being hurt, of making a fool of herself, being made a fool of...

And now by him. She couldn't begin to guess why, except that it must have been a conscious decision. Maybe she was misjudging him, but she didn't believe he was the kind of man to put anything important on hold simply to answer the telephone.

Clearly she wasn't that important.

It was probably just as well. Losing her head over a man who wouldn't remember her name a week from now wasn't smart.

And she had always been smart.

Mostly.

She needed no help to get up but she took his hand anyway, just for the pleasure of touching him one more time. For the life affirming warmth of his fingers as they gripped hers before pulling her to her feet. And she wouldn't have been human if she hadn't been hoping for a repeat of what had happened in his dressing room.

He did seem to take every opportunity that offered itself, the slightest excuse, to kiss her.

The phone stopped ringing but he didn't pull her into his arms. It seemed a pity when she was getting to enjoy it so much. If she were bolder, she could kiss him...

He took a step backwards before the thought could take hold, almost, she thought, as if he wanted to avoid any possibility of a close encounter with the front of her pyjamas. And there was the expensive crunch of Waterford glass being crushed beneath his feet.

He glanced down, not at the glass but at her feet, and before she could blink he bent and caught her behind the knees, scooping her up into his arms. With one hand she clutched at the bowl. With the other she made a grab for his shirt collar as he carried her inside, her fingers curled against his collarbone, her cheek against the straining sinews of his neck.

He held her for longer than seemed strictly necessary considering the thickness of the carpet, the total lack of glass, the sheer effort involved—she was not one of those stick insect girls he favoured.

Not that she was complaining.

And the thought crossed her mind that he wasn't going to put her down, that having swept her off her feet, literally, he was going to carry her straight through to her bedroom. That he was going to finish what he'd started with her buttons, continue his raid on her senses, make love to her with the kind of passion that would sweep away any thought of protest, absolving her of the responsibility of making the decision...

Then he let go of her legs, held her steady as she slid down his chest, his washboard flat stomach, his thighs.

And confronted the reason why he'd stepped back, put some distance between them...

He grinned and said, 'Strawberries always do that to me.'

'Ditto,' she managed through a throat apparently stuffed with cobwebs. 'At least, I didn't mean *that* exactly...'

Not that at all, but an opposite and answering need. A hollow ache that was as natural as breathing and ensured the perpetuation of the human race...

The grin faded, his blue eyes darkened

and for a moment anything might have happened. Even as she longed for it to happen, willed it to happen, he took a long shuddering breath that shivered through her and said, 'Promise me that you won't wander out there in your bare feet again.'

It occurred to her that unless she promised he was going to keep her locked in the circle of his arms. For a moment she considered testing the idea.

'I'll clear up the glass—' he said, taking her answer as read and releasing her '—but you know how it is. One piece always gets missed.'

'Always,' she agreed. Then, because she couldn't think of another thing to say, she offered up the strawberries and said, 'Do you want to take these home with you?'

'I thought we'd already decided they were for sharing.' Then, releasing her, he glanced at the phone. 'Why don't you try 1471 to see who called?'

She stirred. 'If it was my mother she'll assume she got the number wrong and ring again in a minute or two.'

'And if it wasn't your mother?'

'A double-glazing salesman having a hard night?' she offered.

Or Sophie, returning her call. And, feeling suddenly horribly guilty, she shivered.

'You're cold.'

About to say that it wasn't the temperature that was the problem, she thought better of it. 'I'm fine, really.' But that was a lie. She wasn't fine. She was fairly sure she wouldn't be fine for a very long time.

'Pity about the Scotch,' he said.

No, the pity was that he didn't still have his arms around her, that someone had chosen that moment to telephone, that she was a coward and had cut and run earlier...

Except, of course, it had to be that way. How could she possibly make love with a man to whom she'd lied? And she couldn't possibly tell him the truth, not without talking to Sophie first.

'I'd better go and put these in a couple of dishes,' she said, backing towards the kitchen. Then, with a shrug, 'The other way is a bit messy for Lady McBride's sofa.'

It would, however, be absolutely perfect in bed...

She turned and fled to the kitchen, found a couple of bowls and shared out the remainder of the strawberries and cream between them with trembling hands, reminding herself that she didn't have thoughts like that.

At least she hadn't.

She couldn't believe how boring her life had been until she'd met Richard Mallory.

And it got more exciting by the minute. When she returned, Rich was looking at the screen of her laptop.

This time the shiver was something quite different. It wasn't borne out of excitement, or anticipation, or an edgy fear of risk. It was a response to the queasy apprehension of discovery.

She'd left it on and all he had needed to do was touch the mouse for it to come out of sleep mode. How long had she been in the kitchen? Long enough for him to find the email she'd sent to Sophie with his document attached?

'You weren't fooling, you really did try to work,' he said.

She swallowed, glanced at the screen. He was looking at her notes. 'Oh, yes.'

'Fascinating stuff.'

That was it? No outraged accusation?

Of course not. There was no way he could know what she'd done without checking her server and he hadn't had time for that—had he? How long had she been wool-gathering in the kitchen? No. It was okay. He'd be demanding explanations, retribution, the long arm of the law…

And he wasn't doing any of those things. Why would he look, anyway? There was no reason for the judder of nerves that made the bowls rattle against the low table as she put them down. Only a bad conscience.

She realised he was waiting for some response.

'Not that fascinating,' she said. 'I couldn't seem to, um, concentrate.'

'No,' he said. 'Concentration eluded me, too.' He glanced at her. 'I wonder why?'

Now, Ginny told herself. Get it over with. Own up and tell him…

'It's been a difficult day,' she said. That, at least, was the truth. As much of it as she could part with while Sophie was depending on her, anyway, she told herself as she back-pedalled away from the chasm of mendacity yawning at her feet.

She might be short of experience on this kind of thing, but she knew that deception was a bad start to any kind of relationship. And a bad end, too.

But the truth wasn't hers to tell.

In an attempt to change the subject, she

opened the McBrides' well-stocked drinks cabinet. 'Would you like another drink?' she asked brightly.

Madness. She should be feigning tiredness, her heavy workload, anything that would persuade him to take his disturbing presence back to his own apartment. And this time she would shut the French windows. Lock them. Never open them again…

The fact that she didn't want him to go, ever, was an awfully good reason to make sure they never met again.

He was a danger to her peace of mind. Had been from the moment she had first set eyes on him. The phrase 'lust at first sight' hovered just out of sight, on the edge of reason…

Richard turned from the laptop and looked at her. 'House-sitter's perks?' he said, but with a smile that sent the lust factor up a couple of notches.

Never had 'peace of mind' looked so unattractive.

'I'll replace it,' she said.

'No, I will. But only if you'll join me.'

'Then I'll never get any work done tonight.'

'No.' The silence could have lasted no

more than a heartbeat. It felt like for ever. 'Tell me that you really want to work and I'll leave you to it.'

There was only one possible answer to that. She knew it and she was certain that he did, too.

'I really want to work, Richard.'

He crossed to her, took her hand. 'In that case, I'll take a rain check on the drink.' He bent to kiss her gently on the cheek. 'I'll clear up the glass in the morning, when it's light enough to make sure I get it all. Don't work too late.'

And, before she could even think of a reply, he was striding out through the windows. There was a rustle as he took the short cut through the hedge, the dull clunk as he shut his French windows and then nothing.

She stood there for a moment, scarcely able to believe that he'd taken her at her word. Men weren't supposed to do that! They were supposed to tease a little, use their powers of persuasion to get a girl to change her mind. Weren't they?

How come she'd got so lucky?

Was he really not interested?

Once, twice even, he might have kissed her out of curiosity, or because the opportunity presented itself, or because...well, just because. Three times suggested something more.

It wasn't as if she'd fallen into his lap this time. She'd been on the other side of the hedge and he'd made all the moves. Her hand strayed to the button he had undone. She would never forget the way he'd been looking at her when she'd opened her eyes...

Never forget the moment she'd been sure that he was as interested as a man could get.

Yet he'd walked away because she'd told him that was what she wanted.

Could it be that simple? That he was actually a lot nicer than anyone, including Sophie, had given him credit for? Or could it be that he was a really old-fashioned guy who didn't believe in taking things too far on a first date...?

For a minute the idea appeared funny. Then she sat down abruptly, her hands over her mouth.

She'd met him just that morning, for heaven's sake! And there had been no 'date'. Just a series of encounters, none of them arranged. None of them intended or looked for. Quite the opposite.

And all of them ending, or beginning, in exactly the same way. With the kind of intimacy that she avoided at all costs. Except that she hadn't been avoiding it just now. She'd been rushing headlong towards it until he'd made all the right noises and given her the breathing room she clearly needed.

The shattering noise of the telephone made her jump. This time she scrambled to answer it. Anything—even a night of her mother's radical political opinions—would be better than dealing with the uncomfortable realisation that she had been willing, eager, absolutely panting to spend the night with her next-door neighbour on the most minimal acquaintance.

Rich closed his French windows and locked them. Locking himself in rather than the world out. Not quite trusting himself to stay on his side of the hedge. Never had walking away from a woman been quite that difficult.

Or quite so wise.

Except, of course, he wasn't walking away. He'd be there tomorrow, clearing up the broken glass as he'd promised...

And it was quite possible that Ginny might ask him in for breakfast.

He might even say yes. But then he'd have to ask her what she was doing with the draft for Mallory plc's annual company report on her computer. It was hardly a state secret since it had been published a couple of months ago, but even so it was clear evidence that she'd been up to no good the minute he'd left the apartment.

But why had she stolen it? And, even weirder, why had she emailed it to Sophie Harrington? All either of them had to do was phone the PR department and they'd have been sent a copy.

It could hardly have been a mistake...

The program disk couldn't have been more clearly labelled. It would have taken an idiot to overlook it. And Ginny Lautour, whatever else she might be, was no idiot.

He was reserving that role for himself, apparently.

Right now though the light was flashing on his answering machine, reminding him that he, too, had a reputation for putting work before pleasure. At least amongst those who knew him well. Perhaps he should try living up to it.

There were two messages, the first from Marcus, asking him to call back. Remembering the emails he hadn't bothered to open, he hit the fast dial to the computer lab, hoping he wouldn't get an answer.

The phone rang twice and was picked up. 'What the hell are you doing in the office at this time of night?' he demanded.

'You're a fine one to talk, Rich. But thanks to your all night stint, the program is now up and running like a dream so we're just off to the pub to get some grub and a pint by way of celebration. You can join us if you've got nothing more exciting to do.'

'Us?'

'Me and Sophie. She's a hopeless secretary but she makes great coffee.'

From somewhere in the background he heard a yell of anguish.

Sophie?

'Sophie?'

'Sophie Harrington. New girl. Very decorative. Every office should have one. Ouch!'

'So why haven't I met her?'

'Because I've been doing my best to keep her out of your way. I've got the looks but not the money to compete with you. Not that it's made any difference. She's only interested in one thing. Work.'

'Don't go to the pub, Marcus. Bring Miss Harrington here and we'll celebrate in style.'

'Well, actually...'

'It's on her way home. Take a taxi. Now.'

The other call was from his sister, thanking him for the flowers, trying to get him to change his mind about coming down for the weekend. 'Bring a girl,' she said. 'The more the merrier.'

Now there was a temptation. What would his sister make of Ginny? Rather a lot, he thought.

Marcus was right. Sophie Harrington was very decorative. And he was probably right about money, too. Tall, slender, blonde, her hair had been cut by someone who would charge telephone numbers and her clothes had the understated elegance that went with designer labels; she screamed high maintenance and unless he made Marcus a director he wouldn't be able to afford her.

And he was inclined to agree with the porter. She didn't look as if she'd have a thing in common with Ginny.

'Sophie, do come in.' He blocked the way as Marcus attempted to follow her.

'There's an excellent pizzeria just across the square,' he told him.

'What?'

'Take your time.'

He ignored the well-deserved glare and closed the door, guiding Sophie through to the living room.

'I understand that we're neighbours,' he said. Her eyes widened nervously. 'Please, make yourself comfortable.' She looked anything but comfortable as she folded herself up into one of his armchairs. 'Can I get you a drink?'

'Just water. Please.'

He fetched her a glass, considered reacquainting himself with the single malt but thought better of it, and instead sat opposite her. 'We haven't got long.' If he was Marcus he'd bribe the pizza guy to jump the queue and make it snappy. 'Do you want to do this the hard way or are you just going to tell me what's going on?'

Unlike Ginny she didn't flush. She went white and said, 'Oh, knickers.' He made no comment. 'Look, whatever happened, Ginny isn't to blame, okay?'

'I rather suspected that. Why don't you tell me exactly what she's supposed to have done?'

'Nothing!'

'You're going to have to do better than ''nothing'',' he said. 'If you don't want me to call the police.'

'You wouldn't!' She groaned, put her face in her lap. 'Ginny's going to kill me.'

'I doubt it.' He thought of the way her lower lip had trembled when she had seen him at her computer and had to fight down a smile. 'She didn't strike me as having the killer instinct.'

She looked up. 'You've met her already? She didn't say. When?'

'The way we do this, Sophie, is I ask the questions. You answer them. And I'd really like to have the whole story before Marcus gets back with your supper.' If he attempted to send him out on some other pretext he was likely to get a black eye. 'That way you can take your supper, and a rather fine bottle of wine, downstairs to number seventy and continue your celebration in private.'

Sophie looked at him for a moment and decided to talk.

'I was in Wendy's office the day your sister phoned. Inviting you for the weekend? Her wedding anniversary?'

Rich said nothing.

'Wendy said you wouldn't go. She said that you weren't into happy families.' Then, apparently unnerved by his continued silence, 'She said it, not me...'

Since silence was working so well, he kept it up.

'She said that you only dated women who presented no risk. Women you would never fall in love with because they were all exactly like some girl who'd given you a hard time once.'

Tall, thin, self-obsessed. Only the hair colour changed.

'What else did she say?'

'Look, I don't want to get her into trouble. She was really sad about it, okay?'

'And?'

'And nothing. She said what you really needed was a good old-fashioned girl next door. Someone a bit, well, less like your average supermodel. And I thought, well, Ginny fits that description.'

'Good. Old-fashioned. And next door.'

'Umm.'

'And by no stretch of the imagination average.'

She swallowed. 'Yes.' Then, 'No.' And then he saw her relax. 'How clever of you to realise that so quickly. And she's had a pretty ropey time of it too, with her crazy mother. I mean, who would ever call their daughter…?'

She stopped.

'Iphegenia?' he offered, filling in the gap.

'She told you.' And Sophie Harrington's face lit up in the sweetest of smiles. 'She told you her ridiculous name.'

'I believe she was attempting to impress me with her, um, probity. Since I'd just caught her going through my drawers. Looking for a key to my desk. So that she could steal a computer disk.'

'No! I mean, there wasn't a disk to steal. I made all that up, for heaven's sake. I mean, come on, you're Mr Security…' Then, 'She didn't manage it, did she?'

'Not without a little pointing in the right direction. I wanted to know what she was up to. Who was behind it all.'

'Guilty as charged, guv. I just wanted her to meet you, talk to you.'

'Wouldn't it have been wiser to wait until we met in the lift?'

'Oh, please! She'd have hidden behind those hideous spectacles she insists on wearing.' Then, with rather more perception, 'And, since she's not some willowy babe, you'd have let her.'

'Probably,' he admitted.

'Definitely,' she replied. 'You have to talk to Ginny... Why didn't she tell me you'd met this morning?' She frowned. 'What happened?'

Good question. What had happened? He'd met a girl with green eyes and hadn't been able to get her out of his mind since.

He answered her question with one of his own. 'Tell me, Sophie, does Ginny have a pet hamster?'

'A hamster?'

Which was answer enough, but he watched her trying to work out what she should say for the best. 'Only the truth will save you.'

'From what?' He raised his eyebrows.

'No,' she said quickly. 'She doesn't have a pet hamster.'

'Thank you.' He got up then. 'How did you persuade her to do it?'

'Once, at school, I had my diary confiscated in class. If the Head had read it I would have been expelled so Ginny volunteered to climb in through the school secretary's window and get it back for me while I was in full view of the entire school on the tennis court. Losing my house singles match.' She lifted her lovely shoulders and said, 'For diary, insert computer disk.'

'And, instead of expulsion, this time she would be saving you from the sack? Is your job that important to you?'

'Oh, please! No job is that important. If I'd really messed up I'd have confessed to Marcus. Not that he'd have trusted me with anything important...' She stopped, aware perhaps that she wasn't doing Marcus any favours. 'Ginny was volunteering almost before she knew it. Telling me how easy it would be, how your cleaning lady always left the French windows open to air the place...' She stopped before she dropped someone else in it. 'Of course, she thought *I'd* do it. I'm afraid I had to lay it on a bit thick. I told her you were a bit of a bastard.' She pulled an embarrassed grin. 'Sorry about that.'

'Don't apologise. You were nearly right. I'm a *total* bastard, which is why, if you value your job, you won't tell Ginny we've had this conversation.'

There was a sharp ring at the doorbell and she got up, put her hands on his shoulders and kissed his cheek. 'I won't tell on you, Rich Mallory. As long as you don't do a thing to hurt my dearest friend, I won't tell a soul that you're really an old softie.'

Which was fine. All he had to do now was to think of some way to get Ginny to tell him what she'd done. Of her own volition.

CHAPTER NINE

GINNY'S mother rattled on about her latest crusade while she made her some supper. It was an easy conversation. All she had to do was drop in the 'Really?' and 'That's shocking' and 'Absolutely' prompts whenever a pause suggested it was necessary, while letting her own thoughts wander where they would.

Apparently she'd been doing it too well. 'I'm glad you're so enthused about this, Ginny. I'm putting together a committee to run this new campaign and I want you on board.'

What?

'I'm a bit busy for committee work, Mother. My thesis—'

'Your thesis won't make a whit of difference to the world. With your genetic inheritance it's time you were out there, moving mountains...' She stopped so suddenly that Ginny's thoughts were jerked clean out of her daydream about the lingering pleasures of strawberries and cream and right back to reality.

'And what exactly is my genetic inheritance?'

'Scholarship, a vision of equality—' she began. Her stock answer.

'I got those from you,' Ginny said. She was no longer prepared to accept her mother's evasions. She needed to know the truth. 'I'd like to know, exactly, what my father brought to the turkey baster.'

'Don't be vulgar, Ginny,' she said, looking at her wrist-watch, getting to her feet. 'I'd better get some sleep. I'm catching the early flight to Brussels. I won't wake you.'

But there was a tinge of pink to her cheeks that hadn't been there a moment before. She'd got her fatal blush from her mother, too.

'There wasn't a turkey baster, was there?' she said, standing to block her mother's escape.

For a moment they confronted one another and then Judith Lautour sank back into the chair. 'No, Ginny. You were conceived the old-fashioned way with an excess of passion and too little thought for the consequences. That came later.'

Covered with confusion, Ginny said,

'But why hide it, why pretend…?' And then reality bit. 'Oh, I see. He was married.' Her mother's silence was confirmation enough. 'You made up the experiment story to protect him.'

'No, Ginny, not him. He wasn't that selfish. Far from it… His wife was, is, an invalid. In a wheelchair. He loved us both, but she needed him more.'

And the truth hit her like a sandbag so that she sat down suddenly as if winded. She was winded. 'Sir George Bellingham.' An eminent physicist, his young wife had been mown down by joyriders, lost the baby she was carrying, and had been in a wheelchair ever since. They had both always treated her with special affection. Always been there when her mother had been away on some crusade or other. Sublimating her passion in support of her 'causes'.

He was her father?

Oh, yes. How obvious it was when you knew. And his wife, she realised, with the twenty-twenty vision of hindsight, must have known too.

Her mother pulled a wry smile. 'Actually, it was a great career move for me. There wasn't a lot of mileage in being a radical feminist if you fell in love at first sight back then.'

'At first sight?'

'Eyes across a crowded room, fireworks, a full-scale orchestra in the head, an instant rip your clothes off moment in the first empty room you can find.'

Ginny swallowed. 'Oh.'

'The sex was okay. Totally permissible in what was, after all, the permissive society. But only as a recreational activity. And only once you equipped yourself with every method of birth control known to woman.'

'Right.' Then, because she didn't actually want to think about that too clearly, 'Even my name was chosen to suggest a loathing for the male species, wasn't it?'

'I'm sorry, Ginny.'

Sorry? She looked at her mother. 'I've never heard you say that before. Never heard you apologise for anything you've done.'

'I realised my mistake when the interest didn't die down. Go away. You'll never know how much it hurt me to send you away to school, get you out of sight so that the whole "experimental child" thing would drop. I tried to make you invisible but journalists have long memories and endless patience. These things always come back to haunt you. I should have told you the truth when that hideous piece appeared in the papers. Told everyone. George said it would only make things worse.'

'He would say that.' Then, 'No, I'm sorry, of course he was right. Do you still love him?' Stupid question. Of course she did. 'Do you still...?' She stopped, really didn't want to know the answer to that question.

Her mother answered anyway. 'No. He wanted to be part of your life. Be there for you. He couldn't—not if we were...' She faltered. Swallowed hard. 'I...we couldn't do that to Lucy. She was generous, understanding, so good... She deserved our consideration. It was the least I...we...could give her. I'm sorry, Ginny,' she said again.

She got up, hugged her mother. 'Don't be sorry. I'm glad you had someone, even if it was just for a little while.'

'Ginny? Are you awake?'

She hadn't slept. She'd spent the night going over her childhood, remembering all the times that George had been there. Coming with his wife to open days at school when her mother had been away so that she'd have someone. The gifts they'd bought her. Her first bicycle. A strand of pearls for her eighteenth birthday. Special things.

She'd watched the dark rectangle of the window turn from the dull red-tinged black that was the best the city could offer, to purple, then lilac. Remembering.

She'd always felt like a freak. But now she knew she'd just been well, like everyone else. And it felt wonderful. She turned to her mother with a smile. 'I was just going to get up and make you some coffee.'

'No, I'll get breakfast at the airport.' She dismissed the offer with an impatient gesture, back to her usual brisk self this morning, although she looked dark around the eyes as if she hadn't slept much either. 'I just thought you should know that there's a man outside in the garden.'

Richard.

And suddenly she was wide awake, her whole body tingling with expectation.

'He appears to be doing something with a dustpan and brush.'

'He must be a new man, then,' she said, hiding a smile. Her mother, as a first wave feminist would certainly appreciate that.

'Who is he? And what's he doing out there at six in the morning?'

She let her head fall back on to the pillow, tingling and expectation dissipating in harsh reality as she realised exactly what he was doing. Richard Mallory was clearing up the broken glass at the crack of dawn to avoid an early morning reprise of kiss and run. She could hardly blame him. How many times could you back away from saying, showing what you were feeling before the question stopped being asked?

Maybe she should ask her mother.

'It'll be the gardener,' she said.

'He doesn't look like a gardener.'

She knew what he looked like. The exact colour of his eyes. The way his mouth lifted at one corner just before he smiled. The way his chin...

'This is the city. Gardeners don't chew stalks of grass and wear smocks in London.'

'Don't be facetious, Ginny.'

At six o'clock in the morning? Perish the thought.

'No, Mother. Hadn't you better be going? You don't want to miss your plane.'

'Yes, I'll give you a call as soon as I get back. We'll talk about that committee.'

Ginny groaned as the bedroom door closed behind her and she let her head fall back on the pillow. But it was no use. Richard Mallory was in her garden and she was wide awake, listening for a tap on the window. Hoping for a tap on the window. Fooling herself into believing that he would tap on the window...

Idiot. It wasn't going to happen. If he'd wanted to see her he would have left it until later so that they could have shared breakfast. She'd dumped the strawberries down the waste disposal but she could always go and get some more...

She flung back the covers, pulled on her sweats and a pair of well past their use by date trainers and went out for a run in the nearby park before the traffic fumes began to clog up the air.

That way, if he did knock, she wouldn't be waiting like the pathetic female she was, for the man of her dreams—any girl's dream—to invite himself for breakfast.

Her run was long and punishing and, feeling virtuous, she stopped on the way home for coffee and doughnuts.

She had the bag between her teeth and

was juggling precariously with the double *latte* as she fiddled with the zip on her change pocket trying to get at her door key, when she heard the unmistakable sound of a door opening on the other side of the elegant lobby.

No! Not now! It wasn't fair!

She'd lived in this apartment for a whole week without so much as a glimpse of her next-door neighbour. Today, when she looked like a limp rag—a limp, steaming rag—and her hair was clinging damply to puce cheeks, fate chose to play the unkindest trick on her.

She closed her eyes, hoping, praying that he would take the hint that this was Not A Good Moment and go wherever it was he was going without stopping to speak.

Or failing that, because he probably wouldn't be that rude, keep conversation to a brisk, 'Hi!' in passing.

'Can I help?'

No such luck. She opened her eyes and there he was standing beside her, a small cardboard box in his hands. Apparently going nowhere.

Her mouth stuffed with paper bag, the best she could manage was, 'Ungst.'

She assumed he would take the coffee

and doughnuts to leave her hands—and mouth—free. She should have known better. He hooked his fingers inside the waistband of her jogging pants and tugged her closer.

A tiny squeal escaped her lips. Shock, surprise, pure pleasure at the feel of his fingers against her bare flesh.

'Cold,' she said when he looked up, straight into her eyes. Well, that was what her brain said. The sound that emerged from around the paper bag sounded more like an anguished yelp.

'On the contrary, I think you'll find that you're hot,' he replied as, without taking his eyes off her face, he hooked out the pocket, unzipped it and extracted the key, then tucked it back out of sight. Taking his time about it.

It wasn't fair. He only had to look at her, touch her, to reduce her to quivering jelly. He, on the other hand, looked utterly cool and collected.

'All that running,' he said. And something about the way he said it suggested that he wasn't talking about the last hour she'd spent pounding the asphalt but something else entirely. And that it was no longer an option.

'My mother saw you clearing up the glass at what seemed like the crack of dawn,' she said crossly, as it occurred to her that there was absolutely no need to continue holding the bag between her teeth and removed it. And, determined to remove the smug grin from his face, added, 'I told her that you were the gardener.'

'I know. She told me that the hedge was a disgrace and that I should get it tidied up.'

She felt her mouth drop open. 'She didn't! She wouldn't...' Of course she had. 'She's absolutely impossible. I hope you told her to get lost.'

'On the contrary, I assured her that I'd get right on to it—' he sketched a salute '—ma'am.' He took the baker's bag and looked into it. 'Just in case you'd rather she didn't know exactly what did happen last night. Which I think deserves a doughnut for restraint under pressure. Apple doughnuts. My favourite. So...healthy.'

'Nothing happened,' she declared, ignoring his teasing.

He glanced up and there was nothing teasing about his expression. 'If that was nothing, Ginny, you must lead a very exciting life.'

Running again. With her mouth, if not with her legs. She'd been running all her life. The only time she'd ever stopped she'd been betrayed. But Richard Mallory wasn't going to take her to bed and then sell the story to the tabloids. And it wasn't because he didn't need the money...

'Actually,' she said, keeping her feet fixed firmly to the floor, 'last night was about as exciting as it's been for me in a very long time.'

'For me too.' She stared at him. 'So, do I get a doughnut?'

'H-help yourself,' she said, then because she couldn't quite take in what she thought he was saying, she turned quickly and headed for the kitchen. He stopped to pick up the box he'd been carrying and then followed her. 'It's a good job I decided on an extra large coffee,' she said, with what she hoped was the most casual manner.

'Me, too...'

Could that possibly mean what she thought it meant? 'Can you find a couple of mugs and share it out while I make myself fit for company?'

'Don't take too long, Ginny.'

She turned back, looked at him, looked at the box he was holding and then up at

him again and suddenly the excited butterflies took a nosedive. What was in the box?

'You didn't have to rush to bring my
dishes back,' she said. It had to be her
dishes...

'I didn't.'

'Oh.'

'The coffee will get cold,' he reminded
her.

She was not convinced that he had the
temperature of the coffee on his mind and
took her time over the shower, washing her
hair with the shampoo guaranteed to make
her hair shine like silk—well, it worked for
the woman in the ad—and blowing it dry
while she tried to decide what he did have
on his mind.

And what was in that box.

Whatever it was, she intended to be
ready for it. With the sexy underwear. Just
in case. Then she pulled on a pair of black
matador pants that Sophie had talked her
into buying and a pale green linen shirt that
hung loosely to her hips.

Somehow she knew, just knew, that the
next half hour would be a lot more bearable
if she was looking her best. She even considered the application of a little make-up,
but decided that would be a dead giveaway.

Oh, and the underwear wouldn't be?

She smiled at her reflection. If he'd got as far as the underwear it wouldn't matter.

Richard was sitting at the kitchen table, licking the sugar off his fingers. 'I was just coming to check that you hadn't been—' he looked up and for a moment seemed to forget what he was saying '—washed away.' Then he smiled. 'Come and have one of these before I eat them all.'

'I think I'll just stick with the coffee, thanks.' The box was sitting on the table with all the menace of an unexploded bomb. 'What is that?'

'It's not a "that" but a "who". Take a look.'

She opened the lid a crack. There was a rustle from inside the box and she gave a little shriek as the bad feeling in the pit of her stomach came up and hit her in the throat. Then it went down again like a high-speed lift.

She'd caught the briefest glimpse of bright, button-black eyes and a flash of buff fur. 'Is that what I think it is?'

'One small and impossibly heroic golden hamster. Like Odysseus, he was lost and wandering. But now he's home in time for a feast.' He broke off a small piece of doughnut and offered it to her. 'Does Hector like doughnuts?'

She swallowed. He knew. He knew she'd been lying and this was his way of showing her. 'It's not Hector,' she said.

'It's not?' He held her pinned in her seat with the force of his eyes. 'What are the chances of two hamsters running loose in my apartment, I wonder?'

Rather than answer, she opened the lid of the box again. The little black eyes gleamed up at her from a nest of straw. Then blinked. Then disappeared.

'Oh… Sugar lumps.' She risked a look at Richard Mallory. 'Where did he come from, Rich?'

'The truth?'

'The truth,' she agreed.

'The local pet shop. And, actually, they were all out of male hamsters so he's a she. Your turn.'

'Yes. My turn. I'm sorry, Richard.' He didn't say a word. 'I'll tell you the whole story, but first I have to make a phone call.' She made a move to stand up, go through to the living room so that she could call Sophie and warn her that the game was up.

He reached across and put his hand on her arm. 'Don't go.' He extracted a tiny cellphone from his breast pocket and handed it to her. 'No more secrets.'

'No.' Her fingers were shaking as she punched in Sophie's number. It seemed for ever before her sleepy voice answered.

'Sophie, I've got a problem. In fact, we've both got a problem.' Never taking her eyes from Richard's face, she said, 'I think I'm about to be arrested for breaking and entering.'

'What? No... Is Richard Mallory with you?'

'Yes, look, I've made a total—'

'You've done fine. Now, just listen very carefully—'

'Sophie, please, this is important.' She was listening to Sophie but all her attention was on Richard, trying to read his expression. 'Really important—'

'When I hang up I want you to reach across the table, put your hands on either side of his face and then apply your lips to his and kiss him. Thoroughly. Have you got that?'

'What?'

'Trust me, darling. You're the academic, but where men are concerned I'm the expert.'

'Sophie, you don't understand—'

'Yes, I do. Perfectly. Which is why I know you shouldn't be wasting time talking to me.' Then, 'But when you come up for air, I want to hear all about the hamster.'

And, about to ask what she knew about Hector, Ginny realised she was listening to the dialling tone.

There was the briefest pause while she digested her conversation with Sophie and while Richard waited, his face giving her not the slightest clue to his feelings.

'You know, don't you? That I made the whole thing up? That Hector is about as mythical as his namesake.'

'I wanted to hear it from you, Ginny.'

'And you will,' she said, her heart beating so hard against her ribs that he must surely hear it. 'But not right now.'

It was an awfully long way across the kitchen table. Instead of leaning across the table she put the phone down and walked around it until she was standing in front of him.

A few grains of sugar clung enticingly to the corner of his mouth and she reached out, brushed them away with her finger.

A small sound escaped his lips and, reaching out, he caught her about the waist, pulled her on to his knee and kissed her. For a long moment she surrendered to the sweetness of his mouth as it plundered hers, wrapping her arms around his neck, leaving herself open to him, trusting him not to hurt her. After what seemed like for ever, she leaned back a little to look at him and, fighting a smile, said, 'Have you noticed that doughnuts seem to have the same effect on you as strawberries?'

'The only thing in the world that affects me like that, Ginny, is you,' he said, his voice soft, thick, like velvet tearing.

'Ditto,' she whispered.

'Then there's only one thing left to ask you.'

She waited. She wasn't going anywhere and neither, apparently, was he.

'How do you feel about spending this weekend with me in Gloucestershire? It's my sister's wedding anniversary. My whole family will be there and I want them to meet you.'

'Me?' she asked and, remembering the champagne bottle... 'Won't I be a bit of a letdown? Surely they're expecting someone a little more glamorous?'

'They're not expecting anyone. I don't take women home with me. I'm breaking the habit of a lifetime with you, Ginny. I only intend to do it once. Will you come with me?'

'Later,' she said. 'Ask me again later. We've got some unfinished business right here...'

And after that she didn't need Sophie to tell her what to do. It all just came naturally as she showed him exactly what she wanted. It was a world away from being swept off her feet. This was what her mother had been banging on about for as long as she could remember.

Total equality.

And what she had finally admitted to last night. Total love.

The marriage of a millionaire was always news. That Richard Mallory was marrying a girl whose own curious background had aroused so much interest in the press at the time of her birth made it the kind of story that was a gift to the tabloids. And the newsmen were out in droves when Iphegenia Lautour married Richard Mallory three short months after they met.

Inside the college chapel, however, it was like any other family wedding. Richard's sister, sitting near the front and fidgeting about her two small girls who, as bridesmaids, were in pole position to cause chaos, was brimming with delight that her brother was finally settling down. She clutched her own beloved's hand and said, 'It's wonderful, isn't it? She's so wonderfully...ordinary.'

'Richard doesn't think so.' He grinned. 'But then, as everyone said when I married you, love does tend to be a bit short-sighted...' And got his ankle kicked for his cheek.

Wendy looked smug, as if she'd known exactly how it would happen. She'd even agreed to hamster-sit while the pair of them were away on honeymoon.

Marcus, newly appointed to the board of Mallory plc, and now given total responsibility for new product development was there only because he was best man. As he kept telling Richard, he was much too busy to have any kind of a social life...

Judith Lautour was torn between two absolutes—the absolute certainty that her daughter could have done anything in the world she wanted—and the absolute certainty that she was about to do just that.

* * *

'Sophie, please go now or I'm going to be late.'

'You're supposed to be late.' She twitched Ginny's veil into place. 'He has to actually sweat that you're not going to turn up.'

'He knows that I'd never do that to him.'

'This wasn't meant to happen, you know. You were just supposed to have an affair, a bunch of fun. Everyone knew that Richard Mallory was never going to settle down...'

Ginny grinned. 'Sorry to disappoint you.'

Sophie hugged her. 'I'm not disappointed. I couldn't be happier for you. All I ask in return for this piece of stunning, if unexpected, match-making is to be godmother to your first child.'

'You've got it. Sophie...'

'Goodness, look at the time. I've got to fly—'

'Richard said you'd resigned from your job.'

'Darling, I tried, honestly, but I'm not cut out to be a secretary. I can't type two words in a row without messing up. Marcus needs someone he can rely on. I'm not that person.'

'He fell for you like a ton of bricks.'

'Yes, well, there's that, too. He's sweet, but not someone I could imagine waking up beside even occasionally. Let alone for the rest of my life.'

Ginny didn't press it. 'What are you going to do?'

'Sophie, if you don't go now we'll be there before you.' She turned to where George Bellingham, distinguished in grey morning suit, waited to do his duty as an old family friend and give away the bride.

'I'm gone,' she said and exited in a flurry of rich burgundy silk.

'You look stunning, Ginny,' he said, once they were alone. Then, before she could answer. 'I have something for you. A gift to a bride from her father.' It was the first time he'd said the word and Ginny felt a lump forming in her throat as he opened the box he was carrying and produced a pearl choker set with diamonds. 'It belonged to my mother. Lucy and I want you to have it. She knows, Ginny. She's always known. She loves you as I do.'

'I...um...' She couldn't speak, but waved soundlessly in the direction of her throat, indicating that he should fasten it there.

*   *   *

Richard thought he would die waiting for her, turning at every sound, checking his watch surreptitiously every few seconds and then at some unseen signal the music changed and she was there, walking towards him.

His breath caught in his throat as she lifted her veil, looked up at him, and he saw her eyes shining with something that he knew was there just for him, something that no one else could see, and as she placed her hand in his he raised it to his lips and said, so that only she could hear, 'I love you.'

And she murmured back, 'Ditto.'

HARLEQUIN®
INTRIGUE

WE'LL LEAVE YOU BREATHLESS!

If you've been looking for thrilling tales of
contemporary passion and sensuous love stories
with taut, edge-of-the-seat suspense—then
you'll love Harlequin Intrigue!

Every month, you'll meet four new heroes
who are guaranteed to make your spine tingle
and your pulse pound. With them you'll enter
into the exciting world of Harlequin Intrigue—
where your life is on the line
and so is your heart!

THAT'S INTRIGUE—
ROMANTIC SUSPENSE
AT ITS BEST!

HARLEQUIN®
Makes any time special ®

Harlequin® Historical

From rugged lawmen and valiant knights to defiant heiresses and spirited frontierswomen, Harlequin Historicals will capture your imagination with their dramatic scope, passion and adventure.

Harlequin Historicals... they're too good to miss!